BY DARK

THE WITCHES OF PORTLAND, BOOK 8

T. THORN COYLE

BY DARK

"I'm...fine." Alejandro exhaled. "That's part of the problem. I can't figure out anything that's actually wrong. I mean, other than the usual state-of-the-world stuff."

"And?"

"And...taking a break from consulting feels too easy. And as if that's not it. I don't know what I need to be paying attention to, and whether it's coming, or it's already here."

Charlie crossed his arms over his chest. "I hate it when you witches talk like that."

That shocked a laugh out of Alejandro. "Why's that?"

Charlie looked at him, assessing him with steady eyes. "Because when you say things like 'something's coming' it usually is. And that means my life's about to get harder again."

"You're right about that, hermano."

Copyright © 2019
T. Thorn Coyle
PF Publishing

Cover Art and Design © 2019
Lou Harper

Editing:
Dayle Dermatis

ISBN-13: 978-1-946476-13-5

1

ALEJANDRO

Alejandro, phone in hand, earbuds in, paced the sidewalk in front of Charlie's store. A supple, black leather jacket was thrown over his usual pressed black slacks and lightly starched lavender dress shirt. A gray- and black-checked scarf wound around his neck, warding off the late October chill.

He barely heard the voice on the other side of the phone. He was in crisis. It was an internal crisis, but it was throwing every part of his life into upheaval.

Maybe it was a midlife crisis? He was forty-five years old, smack in the middle of what he hoped would be a very long, fulfilling life. Really fulfilling. He had a great partner—the sexy Shekinah—a great coven, and plenty of money. But life still felt like crap. So here he was, pacing on a sidewalk, trying to ignore the droning, entitled voice yammering in his ear.

He'd much rather be inside. Charlie's gaming store—Owlbear—was his two nephews' favorite place to go on their afternoons together. He would pick Henry and Joey up at school and they'd walk the three blocks together, chattering at him about one hundred and ten things, all as quickly as possible. Both of them were talkers, which was funny, because they were also big bookworms. Alejandro had been a bookworm—still was—but leaned toward the decidedly quieter end of the spectrum.

The afternoon edged toward twilight. Alejandro loved the sun, but this year? He welcomed the coming winter, with its long, dark nights. It just felt...restful. He needed some rest.

Just as the year leaned halfway between autumn and winter, the neighborhood was in the midst of a transition, too. There was still some light industrial on the main drag here, with old homes on the side streets, but more and more, small commercial shops like Charlie's mixed with swank new cocktail bars and artisan pizza places alongside tire shops and seedy old bars. It was going the way of all Portland neighborhoods west of 82nd.

Gentrification, Moss would say. Alejandro didn't mind it as much as some of his more radical coven mates. Alejandro was a fan of nice restaurants and bourgeois bars, though he'd been known to set foot inside the occasional dive. He just wished gentrification didn't come at such a high cost.

What the city needed was rezoning....

Earbuds in, phone in hand, he barely heard the voice squawking in his ear. "I understand," he murmured. Polite noise to keep the person on the line at bay. He watched his nephews appear and disappear in between the window displays packed with board games, toys, and action figures. Deeper inside the store, he knew, were the coveted Magic cards and painted role-playing miniatures locked inside a clear glass case. He was supposed to be enjoying their excitement. Buying them an add-on pack for their decks, or whatever it was they wanted this week.

Instead, here he was, dealing with this person—rapidly becoming an asshole who wouldn't take no for an answer—on the phone.

"As I stated in my email, I am currently closed to new clients." He was currently closed to *all* clients, but this jerk didn't need that information.

Taking a break. Getting his head together. Or whatever the hell he was supposed to be doing.

Maybe he was depressed. Was he depressed? He didn't feel like it. He just felt...alternately numb and frustrated.

Alejandro looked across the street to the low-slung building that housed Sub Rosa, the Mexican American food place. They served up a decent margarita, plus tacos. Maybe he'd take the kids there. The food carts at the Mercado down the street were more auténtico than Sub Rosa, but it was a little too chilly to eat outside, besides, Sub Rosa also had hamburgers, and the boys usually didn't say no to that.

Then he remembered. The ofrendas should be up at the Mercado. The ancestor altars, covered with offerings, flowers, and candles to light the way for the dead. Maybe he'd take the kiddos to the Mercado after all.

"I have another call coming in. I'm sorry. I need to go. But if you want a referral..."

The guy actually hung up. Good thing, because no way was Alejandro referring this asshole to anyone he trusted anyway. He had to stop with the polite noises.

"Fucking spic!" a voice yelled out from a car speeding past. Alejandro flipped a middle finger at the receding bumper.

"Pendejo," he said, without too much heat in it. The coven and the rest of the community had dealt a big blow to the white supremacists, but that didn't mean the assholes weren't still around.

He shoved his phone into his jacket pocket, ran a hand across the stubble on his head, and sighed. He should get inside. Let the kids pull him into their excitement. But he just wasn't ready. Couldn't shake the sense of wrongness that had crept forward in his consciousness for the last six months, finally coming to a head around the equinox.

It was guys like the jerk on the phone—and the asshole in the car—who'd led to Alejandro's current crisis. Right now? He questioned everything he'd worked so hard for. All the training. All the hours. All the money in his bank account. It all felt tainted now. Badly fought for, badly won.

He watched people smoking outside one of the dive bars across the street. Sometimes he wished he smoked. Instead, he went to the gym four days a week.

So now what? You're a grown man....

"Alejandro? You okay out here?" Charlie stood, half in and half out of the shop, blocking the glass doorway. Dude looked like comic book Thor, and Alejandro felt the usual pang of half-interested lust at the sight of the man whom he was slowly starting to call a friend. Not that he would poach Raquel's sweetheart. She'd rip out his heart and eat it for lunch. And besides, he didn't think Charlie swung that way. Alejandro swung pretty much every way, though his sex drive wasn't what it used to be, much to Shekinah's dismay.

"Alejandro?" The worry in Charlie's voice increased, and he stepped all the way out onto the sidewalk, hands in pockets, Ms. Marvel T-shirt straining over his very impressive pecs. Alejandro only recognized the young Ms. Marvel in her lightning-bolt tunic and flowing red scarf because the alter ego of Pakistani teen Kamala Khan was one of his nephew's favorites.

"Sorry. Woolgathering. How are you?"

Charlie stepped up beside Alejandro. He was of a similar

height, but much broader. "I'm fine. Shop's doing great. But I was trying to ask about you."

"I'm...fine." Alejandro exhaled again. "That's part of the problem. I can't figure out anything that's actually wrong. I mean, other than the usual state-of-the-world stuff."

"And?"

"And...taking a break from consulting feels too easy. And as if that's not it. I don't know what I need to be paying attention to, and whether it's coming, or it's already here."

Charlie crossed his arms over his chest. "I hate it when you witches talk like that."

That shocked a laugh out of Alejandro. "Why's that?"

Charlie looked at him, assessing him with steady eyes. "Because when you say things like 'something's coming' it usually is. And that means my life's about to get harder again."

"You're right about that, hermano."

Charlie clapped him on the back. "Let's go inside. Your nephews are building quite a stack on the counter. You may need to do triage."

Charlie pulled the glass door open again, a phaser sounded, and Alejandro followed him on through.

Whatever may or may not be coming? It would have to wait. His sobrinos were the priority of the evening.

2

____

SHEKINAH

The oak floors felt cool beneath the balls of her bare feet. Shekinah stood in a sea of white, breathing. Her hands were in what should have been an awkward position, resting on top of her shoulders, elbows splayed out like wings. But it wasn't awkward. Nothing in her life had ever felt so right.

Her teacher stood at the front of the room, hairline receding from his brown face, gray and brown beard straggling down the front of the white tunic covering his round, powerful belly. He was second-generation American who still had family in Delhi. The rest of the room was filled with people like her. Not Indian. Not Pakistani. Not even second- or third-generation Indians or Pakistanis. Americans dressed in white clothing. Brown. Asian. Black. White.

But who was she kidding? It was Portland, Oregon, so mostly white. But in this room, none of that mattered. In this room, there was only breath and sound, movement and the moment.

"Sat!" said her teacher, his clear voice cracking like a retort. "Nam!"

Shekinah rocked her torso, feeling the muscles at her side catch her just as her head snapped to the right. Sharp inhalation through the nose. "Sat!" Her voice was loud, attempting to match the energy of her teacher's, echoing with the others in the spacious room. She turned again, muscles catching her trajectory as her head snapped left. Sharp exhalation through the nose. "Nam!"

The Gurmukhī words reverberated through her body and into the surrounding room.

The Name of Truth. The true self. The soul in alignment with the limitless God. The limitless God itself.

Every breath. Every movement. It was all a prayer. A prayer of the body to clarify the heart and mind. Breath was the practice. Where breath flowed, energy followed. She was learning that. As the moving and chanting increased in tempo, she allowed her body to simply be. To join with the prayers of the others.

Simplicity. Power. For the first time in her life, Shekinah felt like she could simply be. All her worries fell away here, in this room, dressed in white, the culmination of all colors of the rainbow on the light spectrum. Here, she could truly be Shekinah, the pure light of the Holy Presence.

Here, she could be a reflection of the limitless essence of God.

"Sat! Nam! Sat! Nam!"

There was no truth but truth. And it was there, in every moment.

"Sat! Nam! Sat! Nam!" Shekinah breathed and twisted and shouted out the Truth. The spiritual fire generated by the practice filled her body and purified her mind.

And then it was done. The bodies around her stilled. She stilled, heart pounding, breath moving deeply and evenly through her nostrils to her lungs and back again.

Shekinah felt lighter, as if a burden had been lifted from her heart.

It made her wonder what burden she'd been carrying.

"The body knows what the mind won't tell us," her teacher sometimes said. She could feel her blissed-out brain beginning to tick back over into figuring-out mode. Her default, despite her best efforts.

"Shekinah! Do you have time for a cup of tea next door?"

It was Tish, her best friend at the Portland Shiva Society. A younger Black woman with a neat cap of light brown curls and a smile that could melt solid honey, Tish seeped goodness from her pores. Oh, Shekinah knew Tish had problems, just like everyone, but she never seemed to let it get her down.

"Hello!" The two women shared a slightly sweaty embrace. "Actually, I can. Alejandro is busy with his nephews tonight."

"That's so sweet. Let's..."

Shekinah looked toward the door. Yogi Basu stood, chatting with three other students, but as she looked, he smiled and beckoned her over.

"I'll go get our coats," Tish said. "Meet you in the changing room?"

"Sure. Thanks."

The other students left, giving Shekinah a little wave.

"Yogi Basu." Palms together, just beneath her chin, Shekinah bowed her head. When she raised it again, he was studying her, deep brown eyes steady as a flame.

"Have you given our conversation any thought?" he asked. Shekinah swore it was as if the man stood perfectly still, even though, as a former dancer, she knew that wasn't possible. Breath and heartbeat alone made the body move.

"I have, but I don't have an answer for you yet," she replied.

He pointed one long finger toward her breastbone. "You know, I think. Inside. But go meet with Patricia. You both need something from each other."

"Yes, teacher. Thank you."

She scurried out to where Tish waited with their coats, one red, one black, both incongruous against Tish's white clothing.

"Thanks." They quickly pulled on their coats, and in minutes were out on the sidewalk in front of the small Craftsman, just north of the dormant cinder cone of Mount Tabor. The café was half a block away, at the cusp between the residential part of the street and the brightness of shops further down.

Bells chimed as they entered the tea shop, which was fragrant with cinnamon and clove, the scents of autumn. A wooden display case held a few cookies and a single scone. The rest of the baked goods had been decimated by earlier patrons.

Tish and Shekinah both ordered spiced rooibos tea.

"I'll bring the pot out when it's ready," said the weary looking barista.

"Thank you," Tish said, as Shekinah stuffed a couple of dollars in the tip jar.

Divested of their coats again, they slid into a booth tucked near the back of the half-empty café.

"So, can you tell me what Yogi Basu wanted?" Tish asked.

"If you can tell me what the heck is going on with you. You haven't been to class in two weeks."

Tish's bright face fell for a moment. "Can we...I can't just yet. Can we focus on you, instead? That's much more interesting."

Shekinah gave her friend a look. "Okay for now, but I really do want to know." She reached a hand across the table. "I'm interested in your life, Tish."

The other woman shrugged and looked away, before plastering a smile back on her face as the barista approached with their pot of tea.

After thanking the woman, Tish raised an eyebrow. "Well?"

"He wants me to take teacher training."

"That's great!"

"I don't know. It makes me feel...uncomfortable."

"Why?"

"First of all, I don't like people staring at me. Second of all, I haven't been training long enough."

"Ten years isn't long enough?"

"Not for spiritual practice!"

Tish waved a hand in the air and poured fragrant tea into their cups. "Fine. What's third of all?"

Shekinah looked down. "You'll say it's stupid."

"How do you know?"

"Because the two other people I've talked to about this have said it's stupid."

Tish just waited, blowing on her tea to cool the surface.

"I'm a white woman. And I don't feel right about teaching yoga."

"But..."

"I know. I know. Yogi Basu is American and teaches Americans, and I can go to India for more training if I want to, and as long as I respect the practice and the vedas...I've heard it all, but it still makes me uncomfortable. For goodness sake, I'm even blond!"

Tish rolled her eyes at that. "Do you feel uncomfortable when Dennis leads? Or Kate?"

"No. But that's them. Yogi Basu asked them and they said yes. That's fine. But it's not me. I'm the one who would have to explain it to myself, and to my Mexican American boyfriend, and..."

"And those radical witchy friends of his."

"Yeah, them."

Shekinah allowed herself a grin and took a drink of tea. Warm. Spicy. Delicious. She practiced several types of yoga—the Shiva Center trained people in three different forms—but kundalini practice was the one that resonated with every part of her being. It was the form Yogi Basu wanted her to teach. But as long as there was this conflict in her heart...she didn't see how it was possible.

Cultural appropriation was real. She was a white Jewish woman who'd come at yoga via the New Age festival scene, of all places. She'd seen the misuse of the culture and traditions and didn't want to contribute to it.

"Okay. I spilled, and I know you're going to sit here and tell me all the good reasons I should teach kundalini yoga. I'll humor you. Tonight. But someday soon, I really want to know what's up."

"It's nothing, really."

But Shekinah felt it in her bones. Unlike the True Presence, who was both Nothing and Something at the same time, this thing with Tish?

It wasn't nothing at all.

3

ALEJANDRO

Alejandro dropped his keys in the bowl on the nice side table in his condo's entryway. Much as he loved Raquel and Brenda's classic old Portland houses, he appreciated his low-maintenance condo even more. As he walked through to the living room, he thumbed his phone open. Pressed a few buttons. The sound system began to softly play Apocalyptica's second album. The walls were white, hung with Michoacán weavings, a couple of wooden masks and, over the gas fireplace, a flat screen television. Centered around the fireplace, a dark brown leather couch was grouped with a wood coffee table and two squared-off, white–linen-covered chairs.

As the rock cello hummed through the space, he walked past the wood dining table—another sleek, mid-twentieth-century piece—toward the tidy kitchen space. This was all sea-green glass subway tiles, white countertops, and chrome. Opening one of the navy-blue cabinets, his hand hovered in front of a small array of bottles of high-end liquor. Tequila? Or whisky? His fingers landed on a bottle of very good scotch. Oban. One of his favorites. So, whisky it was.

He poured two fingers into a heavy, squat tumbler and went back to the living room, to a corner nook flanked by two tall bookcases filled with curios, a Christmas photo of his sister, Catarina, and his nephews, dark hair covered by silly Santa hats, one of him and Shekinah at the ocean, and a larger portrait from his parent's twenty-fifth wedding anniversary. And, of course, books. Set into the corner nook were his favorite mid-century pieces: a canted wooden chair slung with leather and a matching ottoman, with a sculptural sweep of steel suspending a lamp directly over the chair. Perfect for reading.

Or brooding.

He flicked on the lamp and swung into the chair, shifting the ottoman with his feet until it was just right.

He and Shekinah had talked about getting a place together, around six months after they started dating. But he had weaseled out of it, not wanting to move. He asked if she'd ever want to move into his condo.

"Look at this place, Alejandro. There's no room for anyone other than you here."

The condo had plenty of space for two people, but she was right. It was his place, through and through. There was no room for anyone here but him. And now, in the middle of his stupid crisis, the place felt sterile. Cold. It had always felt warm and welcoming to him before. But now? He could see the ways in which his earlier insistence on ambition and autonomy had crowded out everything else.

He'd bought this place after his last long-term relationship ended. Ten years of love and effort, and they still broke one another's hearts. They had tried polyamory and it just didn't work for Roger. Alejandro had always been poly. He'd tried monogamy on for Roger's sake, but couldn't quite manage it. They were at an impasse. An impasse that ended in tears. The fact that they still deeply loved each other almost made the heartbreak worse.

Roger had found a nice man who wanted to live a happily coupled life. They invited Alejandro to dinner once in a blue moon.

After the breakup, Alejandro had needed to retreat. Throw himself into his work. Study magic. Escape into his books and scotch on the days the pain came rushing back. He'd shaved his head to be more intimidating to the corporate masters he worked with, and, he finally admitted a few months ago, to get some distance from Roger, to shave off his old life.

Thank the Gods and Goddesses for his family. They had kept him connected to his heart all those years.

And then Shekinah had come along, like a cleansing wind. He would never forget the first time he saw her. She was sitting outside his favorite sushi place in northeast Portland, laughing with that wide mouth of hers at something her friend had said. She was blond, with an interesting face, and that laugh just killed him.

When he approached her table, she looked up at him and smiled. That was all it took.

She blew through his condo and his life. Shaking things up with her laughter, fresh fruit smoothies, and her yoga. That was five years ago, and they still lived apart. On one hand, that suited both of them. They were at one another's places four or more times a week, but had space and time to date other people, and have what they fondly called their "bachelor nights." The nights they spent alone in their underwear or pajamas, watching movies or reading books, and eating popcorn for dinner if they didn't feel like cooking.

Shekinah had a girlfriend she saw once a week, and he dated around, though hadn't settled on a steady anything other than Shekinah. And lately? He hadn't even dated. His flagging libido was another sign something was wrong. Shekinah thought it was just stress, but it worried him. She also gently suggested that at forty-five, it wasn't unusual for hormones to change and...

But he wasn't ready to hear that, either.

A few months ago, she also tried to reopen the "getting a place together" conversation.

"Why mess with perfection?" he had replied. There'd been a flicker of pain in her eyes, but she'd moved the conversation on. He'd never told her that after Roger, he was too afraid to take that risk.

Now he wondered if he'd fucked up.

He sipped at his whisky, letting the smoky, peaty scotch roll around his tongue before swallowing. The fumes were strong, almost medicinal. But Alejandro didn't think they'd cure whatever the hell was wrong with him.

Here he sat, in his expensive condo up on Broadway, within walking distance to fifty restaurants and bars, an easy commute to downtown, with a partner and family who loved him, but knowing he was a privileged fucker didn't make him feel any better.

I have no purpose anymore, he thought.

::Then get up off your ass and find one, mijo. And where's our ofrenda? Hmm?::

Alejandro shot up in his chair, steadying the whisky glass before it spilled. What in Goddess's name?

::That's what you get for ignoring us. We'll come and bite

your ass, mijo. You better believe it. You should have taken the sobrinos to see the altars at El Mercado by now, hmmm?

Damn. His fucking ancestors. He set his whisky down on one of the bookshelves and ran both his hands across his skull. Earlier, Henry and Joey had ended up requesting hamburgers instead of tacos. He figured they'd go to the Mercado to see the ofrendas some other time.

::Some other time? When? Dia de los Muertos is almost upon us! And where. Is. Our. Ofrenda?"::

Damn again. They were right. He'd barely registered the coven talking about Samhain, and even though Joey y Henry had made some noise about Halloween, he hadn't really registered how late in the month it already was. Samhain was in five days. Dia de Los Muertos was two days after that, so, one week.

Lo siento, he thought.

"My apologies," he said to the empty apartment. Hoisting himself up out of the chair, he thumbed the music louder, went to the hallway closet, and took down a cardboard banker's box. He *thunked* it down on the wooden coffee table, grabbed his whisky from the bookshelf and sat down on the brown leather couch.

Lifting the lid from the box, he stared down.

And saw their faces staring back up at him. Lifting out the photos, some loose, some in heavy frames. They gazed out in shades of sepia and black. Grandparents. Great-grandparents. Indigenous. Spanish. Mexican. Vaqueros. Rancheros. Businessmen. Pie bakers. Tortilla makers. Weavers.

People with real work. Honest jobs. Not whatever the heck he'd been doing the past twenty years. Goddess. He really needed a new job. Or at least a new direction.

These people were his blood. His roots. His past. A

family, for good or ill. Fighting. Loving. Enduring. A thing some people never had.

Running a hand over his face, he found that it was wet.

"I will build you an ofrenda. The most beautiful ofrenda."

::Yes. You will.::

4
———————

SHEKINAH

The morning had dawned bright and clear, though more rain was forecast for the rest of the week. She'd have to get out today, take advantage of the sun.

Shekinah was in the small office next to her bedroom, trying to get through her usual morning practices. The office was one of her favorite places. She spent hours there, listening to music, working on designs. Like the rest of the old Victorian, it had its original wood floors that glowed in the sun. White-painted wainscoting went halfway up the walls, visible where they weren't covered by low bookshelves or tendrils from the riot of green plants her housemate, Patrick, had taught her how to tend. A rolling kneeling chair was tucked beneath an adjustable light table, next to a long, narrow desk.

She sat on a cushion atop a yoga mat in the narrow rectangle in the center of the floor, staring out the window as the sky pinked in the east. She breathed in, first through her left nostril, then the right. Calling up the powers of moon and sun, to calm and invigorate her. The practices, though strange at first, had become her compass rose. The thing that steadied and guided her. But this morning, despite the breathing practice that was supposed to rebalance her in body, mind, and soul, the mind part of her couldn't stop wandering.

Her phone buzzed on her desk. Insistent. A call coming in. She ignored it, and tried to sink more deeply into her breath. Allowing her lungs to expand from her belly upward. Allowing the breath itself to make minor adjustments to her spine. Filling up. Exhaling out. Trying to let her ego go enough to just be present in the moment, the way she longed to be.

There was more to Yogi Basu's request than simple teacher training. Though he hadn't mentioned it the night before, in bringing it up again, he was also asking her a deeper question. A question he'd only voiced out loud to her once, during their initial conversation on the topic four months ago. He said that he felt she was ready to become, not just a practitioner and instructor, but a person who linked with the lineage of the school all the way back to the original teachers. A person who might, someday, pass on that light and energy herself. She was intrigued, but again, *white person here*. Also, she wasn't sure she could or wanted to abide by all of the restrictions. She already didn't drink alcohol, so that wasn't an issue, and had been mostly vegetarian her entire adult life, eating kosher or halal meat only on occasion.

And frankly? She hadn't yet confessed to her teacher that she wasn't just partnered with Alejandro but had a steady girlfriend as well. Yeah. A polyamorous kundalini teacher? That sounded like some New Age joke. And she was serious about her practice. She wasn't one of those people who took a little from here, and a little from there, and made their own American soup from stolen or borrowed ingredients. Yoga practice *meant* something to her. It meant *everything* to her.

Practice had changed her life.

Her phone buzzed again. Another call. She ignored it. She was almost done, and anyone who mattered knew when she practiced. Anyone else? Didn't matter enough to answer for.

She adjusted her posture on the cushion and began the Sat Kriya practice. Twining her fingers together, she inhaled sharply, tightening the belly, then relaxing once again.

Sharp inhale. "Sat!" Soft exhale. "Nam!"

As she breathed and chanted the Everlasting Name, her body, mind, and spirit were one with the practice that fit her like a second skin. The sun was golden in the sky now and she could hear Patrick, rattling around with coffee in the kitchen downstairs. Soon it would be time to finish up. Water her plants. Get to work.

But for now? She pulled her journal from a shelf and began to write. Morning pages. Three pages to clear whatever was on her mind and heart. Get it out so it wasn't rattling around all day, tugging at her as she went about her work. She found that this practice, though one she'd borrowed from writer Julia Cameron rather than from her teacher, helped her equanimity. And lately, she needed all the help with that as she could get.

Things with Alejandro were...strained. He was in a funk and barely talking to her about it. They barely had sex once a month now, whereas they used to make love at least two times a week. And that wasn't just a long-term relationship slump. It had come on suddenly. Something in Alejandro had changed, even before the big stink with his former client polluting the Willamette River had made him finally put a temporary hold on his business. Thank goodness he had a ton of money squirreled away. He'd made more as a consultant in one month than she did in half a year with her graphic design business.

The pen scratched out her thoughts onto blank white paper. If she found a way to get past her reservations about becoming a yoga teacher, did she have enough money to take the time out and get trained? She did, just barely. And of course, Alejandro would help. They were partners. If he hadn't just up and quit everything, she would have just asked. But it felt awkward now.

Just as it was starting to feel awkward not to share a home after all this time. At first, the arrangement had suited them both. Two homes. No worries about whether or not they could bring other lovers by. The made sure to get plenty of time together, but Shekinah had been wanting more. They'd even talked about it once, before Alejandro's breakdown or whatever it was.

She wondered if he hadn't only put his business on hold, but their relationship. And his life.

A desperate knocking sounded from the front door. She slid her pen into her journal and set them both back on the shelf. She heard Patrick moving down the hallway. Then the front door opening. And then Patrick's voice shouting up the stairs. "Shekinah? You'd better come down here!"

Heart pounding, she quickly bowed to the small statues of Parvati, Ganesh, and Lord Shiva on her altar, and then to the small photo of Yogi Basu. Then she grabbed her phone and yanked open her office door. Bare feet slapping on the wood stairs, hand barely touching the painted black bannister she ran toward the sound of Patrick, speaking low. Rounding the corner of the stairs, she saw Tish, red coat buttoned wrong, hair sticking out in small tufts as if she'd been rubbing her hands over it, repeatedly.

"Tish?"

Her friend stood, just inside the door. "I called, but..."

Her eyes were red and she shook so hard in her red coat, she practically swayed.

Patrick stepped back, out of the way, as Shekinah rushed forward and wrapped her friend in her arms. "What happened? Are you okay?"

Shekinah felt Tish shaking in her arms as if she were a dam, holding back a mighty swell of water that threatened to sweep away everything in its wake.

5

ALEJANDRO

He hadn't started the ofrenda, despite the ancestor's prodding. Instead, he had sat, drank his whisky, and looked through photo after photo, image after image, seeking out the stories of the past. He'd read the few letters his madre had passed along before her untimely death at age seventy.

He'd slept badly after that, weird dreams traipsing through his head. Flashes of old scenes from his childhood. His padre y madre, young and happy. His grandfather cooking puerquo on the fancy new grill he was so proud of, the smell of the roasting pork making his mouth water. Abuelita in her garden.

And then the phantasms. The leering faces. The jeering voices, telling him to wake up, grow a spine, do something! The voices shouted so loudly in his ears, he thought they were actually in his bedroom. That had happened three times, until finally, just before dawn, he'd crawled out of bed, belted a robe around his waist, and shuffled to the kitchen to make coffee.

Here he sat, most of the pot gone, looking at the pictures

he'd stared at late into the night. They looked different this morning. Less somber and weighty. More like people who had just been trying to live their lives. Pay bills. Raise children. Have a little fun.

Alejandro picked up his mother's picture in its heavy, silver frame. It was a portrait taken around the time she'd retired from nursing, just seven years before she died. She'd had two good years before the rounds of chemo started. Before the sickness took ahold of her body and wouldn't let go. He had tried to convince her to retire long before that.

"I want to feel useful, mijo," she would always say, then smile her refusal.

"You were supposed to live forever," he murmured to her photo. Cancer had other plans, it seemed. And his padre? He had died when Alejandro was still young. A car accident that left him in a coma for two weeks and then...nothing. A flatlined heart and a spirit escaping on one long breath, forming a ghost above the hospital bed.

At least, that was how Alejandro had imagined it, in his seven-year-old mind.

He had brought the photos to the breakfast bar and was considering where to build the ofrenda this year. He wanted it to be special. Larger than he'd ever built it before. Maybe today, he could go hunting in some vintage stores for just the right table.

"You always want to spend money," he said to himself, as he poured the cold dregs of his coffee into the sink.

If it was going to make him feel better, Alejandro wasn't going to argue with himself. He'd indulged that side of himself as soon as the money had started rolling in. As soon as he figured out that not everyone was as good at IT as he was, and that his brain worked, not only in code, but in encompassing massive systems. That was what people paid him for. His intuition told him where the glitches were, and what was costing the company. His intuition, coupled with his skill and charm, helped him convince people that he was just what they needed.

But hard as he worked, he realized, he never felt as if he was really working. Not like the people in the box. The rancheros and the weavers. Those people worked *hard*, and at the end of the day—and the end of their lifetimes—their bodies showed it. Successful as he was, and as much as his madre was proud of him, he always felt a little bit lazy. A little bit spoiled. As if life had said, "Here, you can have it easy, while others toil."

Even his recent crisis of conscience about his work could be seen as an upper middle class person—wealthy, even, though not billionaire or even millionaire status—throwing a tantrum about wanting more *meaning* in his life.

Except he did. He did want more meaning in his life. And maybe that was an insult to every day laborer or Walmart worker not even scraping by. And maybe that was an insult to his coven, and his friends. And to Shekinah. Who knew he'd been avoiding her.

"Fuck."

::Grow an espina, nieto.::

"And how do I do that? Didn't I take care of madre those last five years of her life? Don't I care for Catarina's children? Doesn't all of that require a *spine*?"

The ancestors were silent, but he heard their answer anyway.

All that is in the past. What are you doing now?

The trouble was, he truly had no idea.

All of a sudden, he was filled with a longing to see Shekinah. To hear her voice. He'd really been messing up with her lately, but he'd just been so damn messed up!

Buttoned down, responsible Alejandro had been acting like a prick.

He picked up his phone from the breakfast bar and hit dial without even texting to make sure she would be there. She was always there. Should just about be finishing her morning spiritual practices, as a matter of fact. Or would she be in the middle of them? The phone rang in his ear. He pressed *end* before voice mail kicked in and glanced out the window, squinting at the morning sun. He honestly didn't know the answer to the question of what Shekinah would be doing in that moment, and after five years, he should, whether they lived together or not.

And wasn't that a sticking point recently?

"Way to go, man. The ancestors are right. You need to get off your ass, stop wallowing, and grow a spine."

Staring at the photos on the breakfast bar, he at least knew how to start. He would go for a run. Check in with Shekinah. Maybe do some shopping for a new ofrenda table and frames for the photos that needed them.

And after Raquel got off work? He needed to talk with her. He needed spiritual counsel and the high priestesses of his coven was the place he needed to get it. Brenda would go too easy on him right now. But Raquel? If he needed her to? She'd totally kick his ass.

He grimaced at the thought, then went to put on his running shoes.

Sound body, sound mind.

Thanks, ancestors. Thanks a lot.

He didn't know himself whether those words were sincere, or sarcastic.

6
———

SHEKINAH

"I can't. It's just... Sit down?" Tish said.

"Yes. Of course!" Shekinah had never seen her friend this way.

"Is there coffee?"

Shekinah glanced at Patrick.

"On it," he said, and padded to the kitchen. Shekinah followed suit. The bright space would be good for Tish. Better than the north-facing living room that remained slightly cluttered, no matter how much she and Patrick cleaned.

She steered her friend into the white and yellow space. Sunlight streamed through the windows, and the round wood table with four mismatched, white wood chairs was illuminated in the center of the white-tiled room.

"Here. Let's get your coat off." She helped Tish out of the red coat, slung it on one of the chairs, and then tugged at Tish's hand until the woman sat. Patrick had poured the two coffees and switched on the electric kettle for Shekinah.

"What do you take in your coffee?" he asked, as Shekinah poured rose hips and dried nettles into a small pot.

"Just some milk if you have it."

"Coconut okay?"

Tish nodded. She looked startled now, as if she was regretting coming. As if she wanted to run away.

"Don't forget to breathe, Tish."

Tish nodded again and took in a shuddering breath. Shekinah watched her friend will herself to exhale, slowly, trying to tap into the practice. Good.

Shekinah poured steaming water into the pot and got a yellow mug down from the pantry. Giving Tish some time to gather herself. She carried pot and cup to the table just as Patrick set a mug of coffee in front of Tish.

"I've got to get ready for work," he said, gathering up his own mug. Shekinah knew that wasn't true. He always made himself breakfast and sat at the table for at least half an hour before getting ready. She had totally encroached on his space by bringing Tish into the kitchen. She couldn't regret it, though. It still felt like the right thing to do.

Thank you, she mouthed at Patrick. He gave an *of course* shrug and was out the door and up the stairs, probably going to drink his coffee in the comfy chair in his bedroom before getting dressed to go out to breakfast and then off to work at the garden store. She herself had clients today, but her first conference call wasn't until eleven. Plenty of time to talk to Tish and do the last-minute prep on her presentation. At least she hoped so.

Shekinah sat with her tea and straightened her spine, allowing her breath to flow in and out at a steady, even pace. Just as Yogi Basu's presence helped her, she could let her presence help Tish.

Tish clutched at her coffee mug, staring past the kitchen sink out the window. It didn't look as if she saw anything at all. Or nothing outside herself, at any rate.

"Tish? I'm here."

Tish inhaled sharply, shuddered, and turned those dark, sorrowful eyes Shekinah's way.

"My brother..."

Shekinah sat, one hand on her friend's arm, waiting.

Tish just shook her head. Gulped down some coffee. Set the mug back down.

"Your brother?"

Tish held her head in her hands and wept, shoulders shaking. Shekinah laid a hand on Tish's back, one hand over her own heart, re-centered herself, and breathed. In through the nose, as slowly as possible. Then holding the breath, suspended in the chest. Light as the air it was. Then out through the nose, as slowly as possible. Holding spaciousness. Open. Filled with the light of the sun. As she breathed, she felt her friend calm slightly beneath her hand, struggling to match the cadence.

"Shh. Don't try. Let my breath soothe you. Let your breath come."

They sat and breathed together, until Tish was able to sit up in her chair again. Then they sat and breathed some more, coffee and tea growing cold, faces turned toward the sun.

After what may have been ten minutes, or half an hour, Tish cleared her throat. Shekinah kept her eyes trained out the window, at the golden maple leaves getting ready to fall at the next hard rain. At the sun, shining on the golden leaves. Hand still on her heart. Breathing, steadily.

"I've been having premonitions. That's what was wrong."

"What kind of premonitions?"

"Dreams, sometimes. But mostly just a bad feeling about my brother. I've had this sort of thing before and...I was worried sick. I tried to talk to him about it, but he just laughed it off."

She gave a short bark of ironic laughter. "Said it was my woo woo hippie shit, and to keep it to myself."

Shekinah removed her hands from her heart and Tish's back. Poured some tea from the pot. Drank the grassy, tangy water. It was still warm.

"So, what happened?" she asked. "Can you tell me now?"

Tish took a sip of coffee. Coughed. Closed her eyes. Shekinah could see her chest rise and fall with the effort to just breathe. To not fly apart at the seams.

Finally, finally, her friend looked at her again.

"I had a vision in the middle of the night. So strong it woke me up..."

Tish's eyes darted around the kitchen, breath coming rapidly, on the verge of panic.

"What did you see, Tish?"

"My brother! He was dead. Lying half on a sidewalk and half in the street. It was...oh God. So terrible. I called him, and he's fine. Told me I worry too much, but I still didn't feel right. I waited as long as I could before calling you. But I just had to talk to someone."

Shekinah felt her heart stop, then start again. Premonitions of death couldn't be a good thing.

Breathe, Shekinah. Stay in the flow.

"I'm glad you came over. Do you want to talk about the visions some more? Do you want to go upstairs and pray? What do you need?"

"I don't know. Do you know anything about visions? Do you think I should talk to Yogi Basu?"

"Talking to Yogi Basu is probably a good idea. But..." Shekinah knew who she needed to talk with. "You know my Alejandro is a witch, right? If anyone in Portland knows what to do about visions, it's his coven. Do I have your permission to ask?"

Tish nodded, then pushed her chair away from the table, and started to rise. "That'd be great. Thanks. But I should...I should let you get to work."

"Wait," Shekinah said. "Just rest here. Let me fix you some food. Another thirty minutes isn't going to kill anyone." She winced when she realized what she'd said. "Sorry. I didn't mean that."

Tish just shook her head. "Thanks, but, I've gotta get back."

7

ALEJANDRO

I n the middle of Alejandro's run, Shekinah had called, saying she needed to see him, as soon as he could get there.

He stopped back at the condo for a five-minute shower and was at her place fifteen minutes later, where he found her pacing in the living room that always drove him slightly crazy. It was stuffed with books and plants and furniture, bright, cheery, and what some people would call welcoming. To him it felt smothering.

Stopping cold in the entryway, door hanging open behind him, he realized why. It reminded him of all the days he spent at his mother's house during the last years leading up to her death. All of that happened right before he met Shekinah. His mother's place had the same, clean and tidy but overstuffed and welcoming feel to it. But in his mind, it was coupled with the scent of acute illness and antiseptic cleaner. Gone were the days when Madre's home smelled of cinnamon and taco meat, or the hibiscus tea she drank all winter.

Shekinah drank those kinds of teas.

He loved Shekinah. He loved his madre. And sometimes he just needed some space. Quiet. Order. Shekinah wasn't always...orderly.

"You're here!" Shekinah turned and saw him, hair swirling around her, and her face lighting with a brief smile before closing down into worry.

He shut the door and turned back to her. His love. His partner. His steady rock. Her long, ash-blond hair was shot with delicate strands of silver, and her long nose with its slightly crooked tip perched above her lips tinted with the cranberry lip balm she always wore. She still wore the white loose pants and tunic that were what he thought of as her "spiritual clothes." What had happened to interrupt her meditations?

He opened his arms and she walked into his embrace. As he held and rocked her, he breathed in the scent of her. That Nag Champa incense she liked to burn. And something green that he couldn't place. One of her teas. As weird as things were for him right now, she still felt like home inside his arms.

"I called you earlier, but figured you were doing yoga," he murmured into her hair. It smelled of rosewater, and, strong as her body was, today she felt fragile.

"You did? I thought Tish had just called twice. I didn't even check." She pulled back and looked at him. "What were you calling for?"

"I missed you. Just wanted to check in. Do you want to tell me what happened?"

"Yes. No. Of course."

She was never like this, his Shekinah. Flustered. Unable to speak. And lately, he'd been the messed-up one.

"Here. Let's sit down."

"No. I need to move. To walk."

He waited while she put on shoes and grabbed her coat, then they were out the door, walking down the tree-lined concrete path to the sidewalk. She tucked her arm into the crook of his elbow as they fell into step.

"Did something happen to your sister, Laura? Your family?"

She shook her head. "No. Laura's fine. She's still on that research trip in Florida. And I haven't heard from my family in a few months. It's my friend Tish, from the Center."

He remembered Tish, a younger Black woman with bright eyes. Vivacious.

"Is she hurt?"

"She's been having visions. Strong ones. This morning she had a vision that her brother was dead. Shot."

He stopped on the sidewalk and a woman walking her dogs jerked their leashes, trying to keep the excited Labradors from running him over.

"Sorry," he said to the woman, who didn't reply, just scowled and moved past, leashes jingling. "What happened?"

"She wasn't sure, but it was clear the vision terrified her."

The wind left his lungs. "How old is he?"

"Twenty? Twenty-two? I don't know. College age. Young."

Shekinah tugged at his arm. They continued down the sidewalk, past bright red Japanese maples and bare magnolias. He had often wondered what it would be like to move to Shekinah's neighborhood. Buy an old Craftsman or Victorian of their own. Fix it up. Maybe foster a kid or two. That had been last year's dream, before he started to question every damn aspect of his life.

Something pinged at the back of Alejandro's skull. The ghost of a memory. A reminder. But of what?

"Can you check with your coven? Think maybe they can help her? I told her to talk to our teacher, but figured you all might know more about visions."

"I'm happy to ask the coven, and to talk with Tish myself. But has she had premonitions before? Is she clairvoyant?"

"I honestly don't know. She's never talked about it before. All I know is something's been bugging her for weeks now, and this morning she showed up, panicking, at my door." She squeezed his arm. "Thanks for saying you'll help. I appreciate it."

It was nice being thanked, but Alejandro had to admit it stung a little that she wouldn't have just assumed he'd agree. Had they grown that distant recently? Really?

They were coming up on the intersection where Shekinah's street met a small commercial section. He smelled coffee roasting and his stomach growled, reminding him he hadn't eaten yet. He bet Shekinah hadn't, either.

"Can I buy you breakfast? Do you have a client waiting? Or can you cancel today?"

She paused and pushed up her coat sleeve to check her wearable. "I don't have a client for another two hours. God, it's only nine o'clock and it feels like I've already had a full day!" She looked up at him, and her dark, beautiful eyes still looked worried. He wished he could wipe that away for her. Carry the burden, somehow. But that's what being human was, wasn't it? Feeling pain and joy, and sharing both, as best as you could.

That's what his ancestors did.

They turned the corner and he steered her toward the coffee shop, grateful it was a weekday, so there shouldn't be a line. It was nice just walking with her. He really hadn't been spending the kind of time he should with her. They needed to get out more. See things. Do things.

The way they used to, before his crisis started.

"Hey," he said. "You asked me about Tish, but is there something *you* need from me? Some more support? I know lately..."

She stopped this time, and cupped one cold hand against his cheek. "This. What we're doing now. Walking. Talking. Going to eat some food. I just...I've been missing you, Alejandro. You went away and I'm not sure where, and I wasn't sure when you'd be coming back."

Shit.

"I know. I'm still...trying to figure things out. And I don't know how long it's going to take. But I'm here now, and I'll keep trying to be. Okay?"

"Okay," she replied, and pulled the coffee shop door open, releasing the scent of coffee, cinnamon, and baking waffle batter.

He watched her go through, feeling half sad and still uneasy. That ghost of a memory wouldn't leave him, even though no new information had arrived. Maybe Raquel could help him with it.

Shekinah turned and motioned him inside. He nodded and followed her, slipping an arm around her waist as they waited for someone to come lead them to an open table.

No matter what was going on with him, he vowed to be there for his partner. And he remembered what he'd said to Charlie. About that thing that was coming.

He shook his head.

He hoped it wasn't this. Wasn't some visions about to come real. Because it felt like Tish's visions were only one small part of a wave that was going to crash over them all.

8

SHEKINAH

It was early evening, and she lay in bed with Maureen, aka Mo. The sex had been hotter than the last couple of times they were together. Maybe they were just due for a super-hot romp, or maybe they both needed to work off some steam. They lay on Shekinah's big queen bed, legs still tangled, sheets a sweaty mess. Shekinah's fingers played with her lover's short brown hair, staring absently, eyes shifting from the pale yellow walls to the bright painting of sunrise over the Columbia River that hung above a long walnut dresser.

Shekinah was grateful for the simple connection she had with the other woman. Maureen was just good. Not demanding. Stable. Happy to spend time together, and then go off and do her own thing. Maureen was fifty-three to Shekinah's forty-three, had raised three kids, and lived with her semi-retired husband who ran fishing boats on the coast during season. They'd had an open relationship their entire time together. Twenty years. That seemed amazing to Shekinah. Mo had told her there were years when the kids needed more from them that they had taken breaks from seeing other people, but eventually, their natural polyamorous states surged forward again. They'd mostly had light flings. Shekinah was Maureen's most steady girlfriend in some time.

She never spent the night, but was steady as clockwork, every week except if one of them was sick.

Maureen was a nice break from the current mild drama in her relationship with Alejandro. A nice break from worrying about Tish, too.

Seeing Alejandro that morning had felt good, even though they mostly talked about Tish at first, and then segued into Shekinah's work and how Alejandro was doing not working.

They didn't talk about their relationship at all. That conversation was coming, though. It had to, if the relationship was going to survive. And she could tell something else was bugging him, too, though she had no idea what. He'd seemed even more tense than usual.

Shekinah sighed.

"Something wrong, lover?" Mo asked.

"Just the usual. Alejandro. And I don't really feel like talking about him right now."

She rolled onto her side and pushed up onto one elbow, looking down at Mo's bare, beautiful face. The short, seal-brown hair fell in a fringe over hazel eyes, and a black mole rose on one pale cheek. Shekinah loved Maureen's square jaw. Her whole body was slightly square. Stocky, some people would call it. Strong shoulders. Big round belly. Big, square hips and ass. Shekinah always felt safe in Maureen's arms. Sexy, too.

"Want to run away together?" she asked, teasing.

"Hank wouldn't appreciate that, and my massage clients would have a snit."

"Yeah. I suppose."

"Hey." Mo captured her gaze. "If you need to get away for a weekend or something, there's no reason we can't arrange that. We've been dating for three years now, I think we deserve a weekend away if we want one."

Shekinah smacked a kiss onto Mo's wide mouth. "Thanks, Moester. Maybe I'll take you up on that. But there *is* something I want to run by you."

Mo scooched up on the bed and jammed a pillow beneath her head.

"I'm listening."

"Remember I've told you about my friend Tish, from the yoga center?"

Mo just nodded, and waited. A woman of few words.

"She showed up in a panic this morning, talking about visions. Scary ones. And you know, when I was listening to her, and trying to figure out how to help, I think something else was bugging me. I didn't put it together until I was working on a project this afternoon."

Shekinah sat up, arranged herself against some pillows at the head of the big wood bed, and started plaiting her long hair into a braid.

"Are you going to tell me about it, or keep stalling?"

"I feel weird talking about it. Like I'm full of ego, or fishing for compliments, or something."

"Sweetie, just spit it out."

"Why is it, when people like Tish are having visions, and there are other people at the center who've been practicing longer than I have..."

She fumbled open a nightstand, searching for a hair tie. Her fingers closed around the wrapped rubber and she tied off her braid.

"Why does my teacher want me to teach? There are other people who seem better qualified, you know?"

Maureen sat up, grabbed a T-shirt from the tangle at the foot of the bed, and pulled it over her head.

"Who knows why? Does it even matter? Maybe he wants to get into your pants. I know *I* always do."

Shekinah shoved Mo's shoulder.

"Okay. Seriously. He sees something in you, Shekinah. That's obvious. And you know what? I bet a lot of other people do, too. You've got a...calmness about you. Like, it feels calming to be around you. I bet that's a great quality in a teacher. Also, you're good at explaining things. You've even gotten me to understand your yoga stuff, and that's no easy task."

Shekinah was quiet, trying to take it all in. Slow breath through her nose. Pause. Slow breath out. She tried to sense it, the thing Mo was talking about.... She felt the still pool deep inside her belly. That came from years of practice. But surely other people had that, too?

Mo tugged at the end of her braid. "Don't overthink it. Just accept. Either you'll decide you want to do it, or you'll decide you won't. Or maybe you'll figure out you need more information. Maybe that's what's tripping you up."

"Maybe. But the information I want isn't exactly something I can just go out and get. What am I supposed to do, make an appointment, march into Yogi Basu's office and say 'Hey, I'm in two long-term polyamorous relationships and have no intention of giving them up. Is there a policy around that?"

Mo laughed, a bold sound that cracked a smile open on Shekinah's face.

"That's one way of going about it. Why not? What do you have to lose?"

Shekinah's heart sank. Kundalini practice had truly changed her life. It was the longest, steadiest relationship she'd ever had. And more importantly, it had altered her relationship with herself. She needed the practice.

But did she need the school? It felt like it. Her heart pounded, just thinking of never walking into the center again.

"It feels like everything, Mo. It feels like I might have everything to lose."

9

ALEJANDRO

Raquel sat across from Alejandro, in a booth against a high back wall, padded with some sort of green bonded leather, sipping bourbon poured over one enormous rock. His drink was crisp and clear. Locally sourced gin and soda with a twist of lime. Bracing. Just what he was in the mood for. Charlie was entertaining Raquel's son, Zion, Alejandro's nephews, and a few friends with game night and pizza, so she had the evening off.

She'd probably planned to spend it in a bathtub with a book until he'd called her.

The fancy new cocktail lounge was close to Raquel's work and home, so he'd driven down from his condo farther north. The place was cool, not overly pretentious, with massive glass windows that let in the last of the day's sun as it slowly faded toward darkness. It had super-high ceilings held up by massive beams that had to be seventy years old. Plus, they had a turntable and played old vinyl. Songs Alejandro hadn't heard in years.

Up on deck now was Public Enemy. "Fight the Power." Always a classic.

"Thanks for seeing me." He raised his glass. "To the Gods."

She clinked her tumbler against his. "To the Goddesses."

"And to Charlie, who's taking care of the kids."

Raquel grinned at that. "He's turning out to be a good one, huh?"

"The fact that you found a good-looking guy that I'm willing to hang out with even though he's never going to have sex with me? Plus, he likes tweens? You have strange, magical powers, oh sensei."

"Shut up," she said, still smiling, and took another sip of bourbon. "So, before the expensive snacks that you're paying for get here, what did you want to see me about?"

Always direct, that Raquel. Which was why he wanted to talk to her. If anyone would help him get to the heart of his problems, it was her.

"It's a bunch of stuff, actually, that may or not be connected."

"Everything's connected, Alejandro. We're witches."

He stirred his gin and soda with a glass swizzle stick and looked at the floor-to-ceiling bottle display behind the long, gleaming wood bar. The bartender engaged customers at the made-to-look-vintage leather-backed stools, expertly pouring, mixing, tasting sips with a glass straw. Maybe thirty, tops, he was petite and dapper, dressed in a button down shirt in a martini glass pattern rolled crisply up to his elbows, showing off full tattoo sleeves, and Alejandro could just eat him up. A wisp of light beard on his pale skin meant he was probably taking testosterone and seeing what might grow in. Most dapper dressers wouldn't go around with light tufts of hair sticking out of their chins otherwise. But a trans man new to hormones? It kinda went with the territory.

He was cute. But too young. And Alejandro didn't have

time for that, did he? He felt something stir anyway. The small push of lust.

Raquel cleared her throat, pulling him back to the conversation.

"I'm not sure which thing to start with, is all I'm saying. And I can't see the connections yet. I can barely sense them, but they're there."

"Remember when you first came to the coven?"

"Sure, why?" It had been more than a decade ago. He'd met Lucy at some party and became intrigued when she said she was a witch. They thought they might try dating, but weren't compatible that way, had ended up casual friends and before Alejandro knew it, he was petitioning to join the coven for his first year and a day.

"What was one of the first things we told you?"

He took a drink, casting his thoughts backward.

"Don't try to start in the perfect place. Just start. We do magic from where we are, not where we think we ought to be."

A server came with their food. Grilled jicama and asparagus. Kobe beef kebabs. Mushrooms stuffed with sorrel. It smelled amazing and looked even better.

They thanked the server and Raquel dragged a kebab onto her small white plate.

"So just start anywhere, tell me everything you can, and we'll see what the patterns are." She worked a piece of beef from a skewer with her fork, popped it in her mouth, and rolled her eyes. "This. Tastes. So. Good. You can buy me fancy snacks anytime."

"First of all, there's the situation with work. My midlife crisis or whatever it is. I'm questioning everything, wondering if my whole life has been a mistake, and wondering what in the world I'm going to do with the rest of it."

"Do you feel you've done active harm with your work?"

Alejandro bit into a mushroom and shrugged as the flavors of garlic, olive oil, sorrel, and sautéed mushroom filled his mouth.

"Sometimes. As much as most people who make a lot of money. Depends on what you mean by active harm, though. I mean, I know that everyone does harm, no matter what, just by breathing. But that last client that I had to fire? That was bad. Really bad."

"And you did something about it."

He paused at that, took another drink.

"I guess. But maybe if I haven't done 'active' harm"—he made scare quotes in the air—"have I actually helped anyone?"

"Okay, brother, it's all fine and good to do some navel gazing, and at your age? I get that it's time. But don't let it veer into a pity party, because I won't have it. You help your sister, Catarina, with her kids. You help out people in Arrow and Crescent. I know for a fact that you help keep Aiden's soup kitchen going and partially bankroll a bunch of other small organizations. Plus, you do magic that helps, don't you?"

"I just…"

"Is anything I said just now untrue? Do you really think all the community organizing the coven has done in the past year means nothing? And that our magic has no power? Are you questioning your witchcraft?"

Alejandro winced.

Her voice rose, getting louder, until those last words made several people turn their heads. Raquel didn't care. She was a respected local business owner, and a witch, and didn't care who knew. Not after the shit that had gone down in the last year.

He wished he could borrow some of her confidence.

"I'm not. At least, I don't think I am. But that brings me to the second thing. The ancestors are on my back, and it's not just because I haven't built them an altar yet this year. There's something else they want, and I can't figure it out yet. Also, Shekinah's friend has been having visions. Bad ones. And that feels connected somehow to what the ancestors are trying to tell me."

Raquel put her fork down. "What kind of visions?"

"The kind where people die. Specifically, her brother, who's a young Black man, by the way."

"Well, shit. That's not good. Does she have a history of clairvoyance?"

"I'm not sure. Shekinah didn't know. But when Shekinah was telling me about it, I got a weird ping. Felt like the ancestors again."

"If those are connected..."

He tilted his glass at her. "Everything's connected, for a witch."

She shooed him away.

"If those are connected, I think you're right. This could be bad." Raquel picked up a skewer of grilled jicama and asparagus and bit in, chewing thoughtfully.

"On the other hand, could be nothing," he said.

"But you don't think so."

"I don't. She needs to meet the coven."

"Well, shit. I'll see if I can set that up."

He went to take another drink, and realized his glass was empty, and he was tempted to get another. Alejandro eyed the cute bartender. The young man looked up and smiled.

Caught ya, the bartender grinned, raising an eyebrow. His eyes were gorgeous.

Clamoring ancestors be damned, Shekinah had a date with Mo, so he might just get a little drunk tonight, and flirt with a green-eyed man too young to be interested.

Such was his current lot in life, but at least it was still interesting.

10

SHEKINAH

"Call him," Mo said.

They sat at the kitchen table, illuminated only by the soft under-cabinet lighting, eating a post-sex snack of tortilla chips and a bean dip Patrick had left in the fridge with a note that read "Eat me!" on it. He must be out for the night, because Shekinah didn't hear him in the house. Must've left while they were otherwise occupied.

Shekinah was in a soft, creamy robe with gold flowers woven into the design. Mo had her clothes back on, jeans and a navy shirt under a purple pullover sweater. She'd be driving back to Beaverton in another hour or so. "Home by midnight unless something important comes up" was the general rule with her husband, and they both abided by it. Probably one reason their marriage had lasted so long. They made agreements and stuck to them.

Mo did occasionally spend the night, but that was only every month or so. and that had only started when it became clear their relationship was more than a passing thing.

Mo had a glass of pale lager in front of her, while Shekinah was drinking her favorite non-tea beverage: orange bitters and sparkling water. People sometimes asked her if she missed alcohol, but she really didn't. It was nice having a clear head, and it helped with her emotions, too. Besides, she'd do pretty much anything to help her practice, so, no alcohol it was.

Well, she'd do almost anything. Anything except give up Alejandro and Mo and the life they'd built. It was a good one. If Alejandro ever got through his current malaise and agreed to move in, they could get an old house together, maybe in this neighborhood. Patrick would have no shortage of people wanting to move into this place. It was a great deal, and he was super easy to live with. She would miss it here, but... Who was she kidding, Alejandro wasn't moving in with her anytime soon.

"Call who?"

"Your teacher. What's the worst that could happen?"

"He could kick me out of the center. Out of the whole organization."

"Then he's a putz and the school is a bigoted piece of trash." Mo shrugged, as if she was just stating a simple truth, and took a drink of beer.

Shekinah swirled her drink in her hand, circling the liquid inside, ice cubes tinkling against glass.

"It isn't that simple, Mo. There are cultural differences. Religious beliefs. Traditions..."

"And you mean to tell me that you, of all people, are going to buy that? What, are you just going to stop being queer all of a sudden? I don't get you!"

Wow. She might as well have smacked Shekinah across the cheek. They almost never argued. Just didn't have that kind of a relationship. She throttled down a flash of anger and took a breath.

"Why are you so angry?"

Mo shook her head and drank more beer. "Isn't it obvious? Because I love you and can't stand to see you even considering diminishing who you are. I gotta pee."

Maureen shoved her chair back and left the room.

Shekinah drank some water, trying to cool the fire inside. She was angry and hurt, but, she realized, not at Mo. Mo was right. What the hell was she doing? What had she been doing all along, ever since the discussion of initiation and teacher training and all the rest of it came up? She'd been hiding who she truly was, afraid her teacher would reject her.

"You're a damn adult, Shekinah. Why are you still seeking other people's approval?"

But seeking approval was deeply ingrained. If people didn't approve, it meant she might be in danger. At least, that's the way things were in her family of origin. After all these years of spiritual work, she clearly hadn't shaken that past.

Shekinah sighed and took another drink of flavored water before rising to fill the kettle. She needed comfort. Warmth. She needed tea.

She heard Mo come back into the kitchen. Felt her behind her, then felt those strong arms around her waist. She relaxed, feeling the mild hurt of Mo's words fade. Mo rested a cheek against her right shoulder blade and pulled Shekinah closer.

"I'm sorry I snapped at you. I just... You're awesome, Shekinah. And if someone doesn't see that? I think you should say fuck 'em."

Shekinah laughed and flicked the kettle on.

"I'm not exactly going to tell my teacher to fuck off, but I take your point." She turned in Mo's arms. "And thanks for caring enough to get angry. I actually appreciate it. Want some tea?"

"Yeah. I probably shouldn't finish that beer if I'm going to drive home."

"About that... It's not a big deal if you can't, but do you think you could spend the night tonight? I'd like it if you could stay. Help me talk through this some more. Fall asleep together."

Mo looked at her, questioning, then gave her a gentle kiss.

"Sure thing. Hank's got an early start tomorrow anyway. Just let me text and let him know."

She texted as Shekinah fixed a pot of chocolate mint tea. Then they sat back down at the table.

"So," Mo said. "What do you need to think through?"

"How to broach the subject with Yogi Basu."

Mo jerked her head back, surprised. "You're actually gonna tell him?"

"Yeah. You're right. Hiding isn't going to help the situation, so I may as well come clean. Stop tying myself in knots about it."

This, at least, was one thing in her life she could control. How to tell other people who she was.

The rest would wait.

She reached across the table and squeezed her lover's hand.

"Thanks, Mo."

11

ALEJANDRO

Catarina was picking up the kids from Owlbear, and Raquel had left, saying she wanted to enjoy an hour at home alone before Zion got back. Alejandro should probably get home himself, start working on the ofrenda, but he wasn't in the mood.

He felt restless. Wanting to either call up a friend to bullshit and drink with, maybe play a round of poker, or...his eyes returned to the bar, where the snack was still bartending.

Taking his empty glass up to the long sweep of the bar, Alejandro settled into one of the empty leather-backed swivel stools. He bet the place was packed on weekends, but smack in the middle of the week, it was half empty.

"Need to settle up?" the bartender asked.

"I think I'd like another," Alejandro said. "Do you have a favorite local gin?"

"There are a few I like, but since you already had a classic, why don't you try this one?" He turned and reached a deco-looking bottle down off the shelf. "Aviation. It's lighter on the juniper than most, so it tastes lighter. Smoother."

"Great. I'll try it."

"With soda? Or do you want a martini?"

"Martini. Extra olive, please."

"You got it." There was that smile again. Damn. *Too young for you, Alejandro.* Reminding himself of the guy's age wasn't making him any less appealing, even though it should. Plus, he hadn't exactly been paying good attention to his partner lately. Did he really have the bandwidth for this?

Maybe not. But sometimes that's how poly worked. You were in a slump, and a little fresh excitement came your way, pumping more love and lust back into your long-term relationship. It wasn't that you were using the new person, it was that the extra endorphins spilled over onto everyone involved.

Besides, it was just a little harmless flirtation. Right? No way this guy was going to be actually interested.

"What's your name?"

"Thomas," the bartender replied, sliding the martini glass onto a coaster in front of Alejandro. A light sheen of Vermouth covered the surface, and two of the olives were submerged just beneath the surface, the third hanging out near the edge of the glass. The hairs over Thomas's tattoos were pale blond. Barely there. The tattoos themselves were a riot of color. One arm sported a variety of flowers, a hummingbird, and bees darting here and there. The other arm was filled with fruits and vegetables, eggplant, tomatoes, and what looked like rainbow chard.

"You're either a gardener or a cook," Alejandro remarked.

"What? Oh. My arms. Yeah. I love both, actually. I was all set to attend culinary school when the money ran out. I'm taking some time off to sock some cash away."

"Do they offer scholarships to culinary school?"

"Are you kidding me? No. And I had some other expenses come up...sorry. Don't know why I'm telling you all this. Excuse me." Thomas turned and walked to the other end of the bar.

Abrupt. Maybe he wasn't interested in flirting. That was okay, Alejandro got it. The guy was at work and was paid to be nice to people. Alejandro knew better than to flirt with people at their workplace. It wasn't fair.

He watched Thomas talk to a bearded man around Alejandro's age, in black jeans, a white shirt, and more tats who'd come out of the swinging kitchen door. Thomas nodded, then turned to take the orders of a couple who'd sidled up to the end of the bar. It wasn't busy, which worked to Alejandro's advantage. Maybe Thomas would be back.

And maybe you should give him a break. He's at work, asshole. Cassie and Selene would have your head for harassing the poor guy.

Maybe that was part of his midlife crisis. He was turning into one of those middle-aged assholes so desperate for attention they'd hit on people they shouldn't. Vulnerable people. People just trying to get through their workday. People waitressing or tending bar. Airline attendants. He'd always had contempt for those people, and yet, here he was.

Alejandro sipped at the drink. The bartender was right. It was the smoothest martini he'd ever tasted. His phone buzzed.

It was a text from Raquel. *Go home, you idiot. I know you're still there.*

Busted, he texted back. *But I'm not going anywhere.* He probably *was* going directly home after this martini, and going home alone, but he didn't have to let Raquel know that.

She sent back a middle finger emoji and he laughed. It was nice having a spiritual family that could have your back and gave you shit at the same time.

"Your boyfriend?"

Alejandro looked up. "What?"

"The text. I'm being nosy." There was that smile again. And Thomas had a spray of freckles across his cheeks. Damn.

"No boyfriend. I do have a partner, but we're open."

Thomas wiped down some condensation from the bar. "That's what they all say."

Alejandro shrugged. He was used to this conversation. "I don't blame you for not believing me. But Shekinah and I have been together five years and haven't been monogamous for any of it."

And hopefully they'd last another five, or more. If she was willing to put up with him.

"Huh. That's cool. Does that mean I can see you again?"

Well. This situation had moved quickly. Maybe he wasn't an old creep after all. Or not just an old creep.

"I'd like that."

"Hey, sorry about before," Thomas said. "I overshare sometimes, and then, you know…"

"Not a problem. I know you're working. Speaking of, what time are you off?"

"Dan, the owner, just told me I could take off early because we're slow. So another half hour?"

"Sounds great," Alejandro said.

And it did sound great. Whether they went for a drive, or a walk…or back to his place to make out, it really was great.

No matter what else was going on in his life, it felt good to be wanted by a handsome young man. He'd been so lost in his shit lately, he didn't even realize he missed that.

The ego knows what it wants, even when the mind is clueless.

12

SHEKINAH

Shekinah sat at her desk, attempting to concentrate. Morning light streamed through the windows. The day had dawned clear and bright, though she knew the air outside would be chilly, and more rain was forecast to be on the way.

Maureen had woken up way too early and kissed Shekinah goodbye. She tried to get back to sleep but gave up after fifteen minutes. Her brain was too wired to drift off again, so she got up, showered, did her morning prayers and practices, brewed some tea, and settled into work.

At least, that was the plan. But her mind kept returning to Tish's ravaged face, and the phone call she was going to make to Yogi Basu once the hour ticked over to something more reasonable.

Oh, her teacher would be awake, but disturbing anyone's morning still felt like a violation.

She sighed. She had so much work to do and a super-full day ahead. This design was tricky, and the client was even trickier. She really needed to be at home all day, working. But she'd agreed to meet Alejandro at his place for lunch. They needed to talk before they met with Raquel and Tish that evening and she knew it, though the timing wasn't great. There was too much left unsaid right now to talk of other things, but no time to address any of the elephants currently dancing around between them.

Besides, when was the timing ever good for those sorts of conversations? Shekinah had never been one of those people who loved endless relationship processing, and Alejandro was downright avoidant.

She stood and stretched, feeling annoyed with the whole situation, and mildly disgusted with herself. She couldn't help but think she should be doing better about all of this, but instead, she kept tying and retying the same old knots.

"I have *got* to work up some steam on this project. Come to think of it..."

She looked at the small statue of Ganesha, took out a cone of incense, lit it, and set it in the dish at his feet. Then, centering herself, Shekinah took out her wooden mala, and began to chant, the mala beads slipping smoothly past her fingers.

"Om Gam Ganapataye Namaha. Om Vignanaashnay Namah. Om Gam Ganapataye Namaha. Om Vignanaashnay Namah..."

Surrounded by the scent of incense and warmed by the shaft of sun, she chanted until the air around her sparkled and she felt clear and strong inside.

Finished, she bowed to Lord Ganesha, set her mala down, and turned once more to her desk.

Shaking out her hands, she sat back down.

13

ALEJANDRO

He was dreaming. Dreams of dust and fire. Of shotgun blasts in dry, summer air. Of wind moving through trees tinged with red and gold, announcing the arrival of autumn. He dreamed of cows stampeding. Of weathered faces. And of brown hands, passing a wooden shuttle over and under, pulling the threads tight.

Forming a pattern.

Alejandro woke to a firm bed beneath him, cheek cradled in an equally firm pillow. He groaned and blinked his eyes. A weak shaft of gray light sliced the room. He must not have closed the blackout curtains very tightly last night. After...

Very gently, slowly, he rolled onto his back and turned his head. A pale form softly slept next to him on the bed, one arm thrown back, head half turned away from the shaft of light. Thomas had thrown the black comforter half off himself, and he slept, naked, pale pink scars just visible below his pectoral muscles, showing the place where breasts had been.

Last night, when Thomas had swept his white under-shirt over his head, Alejandro had felt honored that the young man would trust his surgery scars to someone he didn't even know. It must have shown on his face, because Thomas had just shrugged and said, "This is part of who I am. Why hide it?"

Why hide it? Had Alejandro ever been that honest about himself? To anyone? His lightly starched shirts and neatly pressed dress slacks. His designer glasses, changed out every two years. His perfect stubble, even. All of it was him, but it was also armor. An act he put on to throw the corporate movers and shakers off guard. They always expected tech whizzes to be jeans and T-shirt guys—they never expected women at all—so Alejandro dressed like the rich, successful man he was. But not in a suit. That would have been trying too hard. He kept his naturally lean body gym toned. His condo was always neat.

Alejandro liked order. And his life was now disorderly. He had no schedule. No work to do. His long-term relation-ship was strained. And he'd just taken home a guy *almost* young enough to be his child, if he'd been the parenting type.

Thomas was just who he was. Alejandro? He was strug-gling to get through the day right now.

And wasn't that a bitch? *At least you finally admitted it. Asshole.*

He waved the voice away, and lay on his back listening to Thomas breathe. The sex had been sweet, and Alejandro hoped it happened again, but even if it didn't, Thomas had already given him a gift. He'd made Alejandro feel alive again. Just present, in the moment, the way a balanced witch could be. Not fretting over past regrets or worrying about the future. Just in the moment, with lips on skin, the scent of a new person's body, the occasional gasps of laughter. And then release.

He was just about to roll over and curl up against Thomas's body when the scent of cordite filled his nose.

"What the—?" he whispered. The dreams. Guns firing. Closing his eyes, he saw the glint of light off a sheriff's star. The star of authority. A badge. A symbol of order.

Just as the witch's star was a symbol of the flow of the natural world. Earth. Air. Fire. Water. Spirit. And the witch's body. Arms. Legs. Head.

Symbols. Patterns.

The weavings. The brown hands, running coarse cream yarn through black, yellow, and red.

Carefully, he lifted the comforter and top sheet and eased out of the bed. Toeing into his slippers, he grabbed a robe from the back of one of two gray wool club chairs that sat against the wall, flanking a sleek black gas fire. He eased the bedroom door open and walked down the dark hallway to the open common space.

Gray morning light filled the room from the big windows lining one living room wall. He walked through the room, clicking on floor lamps, including the sculptural reading lamp, the long sweep of its metal arm dangling a silver orb above the waiting leather sling chair. The light illuminated the books and objects on the shelves. His eyes rested on a reproduction of a Michoacán sculpture. A heavy, square head with perfectly formed features. The ancestors whispered at the base of his skull, prodding him.

"What do you want?" he asked the sculpture. It had no answer for him. But the dreams did. The tingling at the base of his skull reminded him.

He ran a finger along the new ofrenda table he'd found at a vintage store yesterday afternoon. A tall, graceful, mid-century console with shelves above and sliding storage panels below. It fit the room perfectly, just as he knew it would, the stained teak glowing warm in the lamplight. Pleased with his purchase, he'd brought it home with the help of Cassiel's boyfriend, Joe, and his truck before heading off to meet Raquel.

And finding Thomas.

He turned toward the main weaving, hanging from the westernmost wall. A stylized figure, with a triangular body, arms upraised, legs spread in a strong, geometric stance. The square face stared directly at him, eyes fuzzy where the nap of the yarn had worn over the years.

But what called to him in the early morning light were two bright red horizontal stripes, one near the top and one near the bottom of the weaving. He'd always just thought of them as decoration, but the pinging at the base of his skull told him something different. He moved closer, looking at the tight weave of the threads. Was there a pattern here? Or was the pattern the whole small rug?

Alejandro backed up again, trying to see the relationship the red bars had to the whole.

"Protection," he murmured to the silent room. Red bands, one above, one below, protecting the figure in the center, who stood, hands raised to the sky. Was that a position of power? Of summoning? Or of surrender?

Alejandro softened his gaze, trying to see through and around the pattern. Soft focus, a magical technique used by psychics who wanted to observe more than was seen initially, on the surface. There was something...just outside the corners of his eyes. The red bars rippled, and he swore the figure moved its left hand.

The Left Hand Path. The path of shadows. Of secrets. Some said of evil, but that was childish superstition. Both hands were needed to shape a world. The witch brought two sides together, light and dark, hot and cold, day and night. All polarity was brought into harmony by the magician or the witch.

This was a pathway that Alejandro hadn't walked before. It was one, he saw now, that he'd been avoiding. To embrace it meant bringing chaos into his orderly life.

"Well, things are in chaos now, aren't they?" To anyone else, his life probably still looked orderly, but he knew just how much he'd given up. A stack of unread emails from clients who wanted to pay him a lot of money to do what he did best. A stack of unspoken words between him and Shekinah, the love of his life. A stack of barely examined thoughts and feelings that had led him to this...impasse.

"Alejandro?" Thomas called softly from the doorway. "Is everything okay? Should I go home?"

Alejandro turned. Thomas's hair was a tousled mess, and he stood there, barefoot and in his white T-shirt and black boxer briefs, looking oh so beautiful.

What the hell am I doing? Trying to borrow a doorway back to his late twenties, when, confusing as things were, at least they were confusing for everyone around him. At least he wasn't expected to have his life together and to know exactly what came next.

"Hey. Hope I didn't wake you. You're fine. It's fine. I just couldn't sleep." He walked toward the kitchen area. "Want some coffee?"

Thomas rubbed his face and ran his fingers through his hair. "That'd be great, if you don't mind. Can I take a shower?"

"Of course! Clean towels and washcloths are in the cabinet. I'll get the coffee going while you shower."

The younger man padded off, and Alejandro sighed.

He looked back at the weaving, more and more certain it was about protection. But protection against what? And for whom?

14

SHEKINAH

Shekinah navigated her Subaru through northeast Portland. The gray skies were back after yesterday's sun, hovering over the tall trees and muffling the sounds of cars and the shriek of children as she passed a playground. It was the sort of day that usually lifted her heart, but today, being out and about brought her no joy.

She really didn't have time for this lunch. She'd called Yogi Basu to set up an appointment to talk after his class that evening. A class she was going to skip to meet with Tish and the others.

Ostensibly, this lunch was to talk about Tish some more, get the lay of the land before their meeting with Raquel. But really? After chanting to Ganesha, Shekinah got some clarity about both work and Alejandro. There was no avoiding it anymore. At least, not for her. They were going to talk about their relationship. They had to. Both of them had been putting it off, trying to pretend as if everything was still at status quo. Well, it wasn't. The easy time she'd spent with Mo only highlighted the distance with her partner.

Every relationship was different, and that was fine, but

she shouldn't feel more intimacy with the married woman she saw once a week than she did with the man she was supposed to have a deeper commitment to. Maybe it was time to reassess. Let their relationship find a new level, and new pathway. Let some things go.

But she didn't want that. She wanted *more* commitment, and at one point, she thought Alejandro was going to want that, too.

She braked at a stop sign to let a punk dad push his baby stroller across the intersection. A leashed wiener dog trailed happily behind.

Shekinah had no issue with Alejandro taking time off work. He clearly needed to and had enough money to float for a while. What she took issue with was his withdrawal. From her. Oh, she'd tried to work through it in meditation and through prayer, but none of it stuck. Not for more than a few days, at any rate. Every time she saw him was another reminder of the distance between them. She knew she needed patience. That it wasn't about her. But that didn't make it hurt less. That was the thing about having a partner. Even during messed-up times, they were there. You were in relationship together, helping each other work it out.

That wasn't happening right now. A car pulled out from in front of Alejandro's condo building.

"Thank you!" she called out to the universe. She'd take every blessing she could get.

After navigating into a parking space, she turned off the car and just sat for a moment. She looked at the small images of Ganesha, Parvati, and Shiva on her dashboard, and inhaled slowly, as deeply as she could.

"Jai Ganesha. Om Namah Shivaya, Maata Cha Paarvati Devi..." she prayed. Who knew what obstacles were still in front of her? This morning proved she needed all the help she could get with the situation with Tish and Alejandro both.

She texted Alejandro to let him know she'd arrived, grabbed her purse from the passenger seat, scanned for traffic, then opened her door and got out.

"Here goes." She took a deep breath, then unlocked the front security door and made her way up three flights of stairs.

He was waiting for her, door open, smile on his face. "Hey, my love!"

She managed a smile. God, he was beautiful. Most people would call him handsome, she knew. But to her, when he smiled? He was always beautiful. She wanted to forget about the conversation, wrap him in her arms and take him straight to bed.

"Hey there, yourself!" They kissed, a quick, friendly peck at first, and then a slower, deeper connection. His lips were warm, soft, firm. Exactly what she wanted. She sighed and rested her forehead against his.

"You okay?" he asked. "I know this must be a lot for you. Tish's visions and all..."

She walked past him into his spotless, well-appointed condo, boot heels clacking on the dark brown bamboo floors. Dropping her purse on the brown leather sofa, she shucked off her black coat and turned.

"It isn't just about Tish, though that worries me. It's you, Alejandro. Us." She crossed to the tidy kitchen space and filled the kettle for tea. "I wish we could just talk about Tish. Hell, what I actually wish is that we could just hop into bed and make love. It's been a month, you know."

She paused, and tilted her head at a familiar sound. The light scent perfuming the air. "Are you doing laundry? I thought you did laundry on Saturday mornings."

Alejandro was nothing if not a creature of habit. That was one reason this whole "not working right now" thing had thrown him for such a loop.

His brown skin grew ruddy and he glanced down, just for a moment, before looking up again.

"You had sex with someone last night, didn't you?"

He shrugged, a sharp jerk of his shoulders. "I did. So what? Didn't you have Maureen over last night?"

Shekinah rubbed her hands across her arms, suddenly cold. She strode across the floor and flicked on the fire, trying to calm down. Her heart was beating so fast! Her throat was closing up. Do. Not. Cry. Damn it.

"This has nothing to do with Maureen, and you know it! Do not deflect with me, Alejandro!"

He threw up his hands and turned his back on her, heading to the kitchen, crashing cupboards open, getting down mugs. Teabags. He was making her tea.

"Are you going to talk to me?"

"I'm making you your damn tea! I thought you'd appreciate it!" He stopped, both hands on the kitchen counter, head down, breathing hard. "I was trying to buy us a little time. Make us something to drink. Maybe calm down a little."

He looked up at her, dark eyes hurt. Angry. Hers probably looked the same.

She took off her boots, then walked in stocking feet to the kitchen. No more crashing around. She loved him. He loved her. No matter what, those things were true.

Placing her palms against the cool white quartz, she leaned toward him, the counter between them. Close enough for now.

The kettle clicked. He poured steaming water into two

mugs that already held teabags. The scent of mint mingled with the smell of laundry soap. Laundry soap. Damn it.

"I just...are you trying to control my sex life now?" Still angry, but softer, more plaintive, as if part of him was pleading for her to understand. "We agreed..."

"This has nothing to do with Maureen. Or our agreements."

He set a mug in front of her. She didn't want it anymore. She wanted to throw it across the room. Watch it smash and splatter. But she didn't do things like that. *They* didn't do things like that.

"You really don't know why I'm upset?" she asked.

He ran his hands over the light stubble on his head. He looked tired, she noticed.

"I know we've been having trouble lately. That my crisis or whatever it is has been hard on you. But about me bringing someone home last night? No. I don't. It's not as if that's something new."

"It isn't because you had sex with someone else. It's because you haven't had sex with *me* in over a month. You've said you needed space. That you weren't feeling it. That it wasn't me. Well, I've been patient. People go through things, you know?"

"And I've told you I appreciate that. That I appreciate *you*."

"God, Alejandro! Don't you see how this must make me feel? You brought someone home last night! You had sex with some random, casual stranger!"

"How do you know..."

"Don't! Don't. Even. Do. That. You're deflecting again, and that pisses me off. And worries me. You say it's not about me, but you can have sex with someone else all of a sudden? Well, that makes it *feel* like it's about me! Like it's about us."

He looked down again, staring at his tea mug as if answers floated in the pale, fragrant water. "Maybe it is." His voice was so quiet she barely caught the words. "I just don't know, Shekinah. There's so much going on and..."

"Were you ever going to talk to me about it?"

He looked at her, wounded. "Yes. I was."

"When?"

He just shook his head. "I don't know! I don't know anything right now! I thought I was taking time to figure things out! I thought we'd talked about that!"

She needed to be careful. So careful right now, or she'd blow things up.

"We had. But it was my understanding that you'd come to me when you were ready, not find someone else."

"I didn't..."

"I can't do this right now, Alejandro. I'm too angry. We're both going to say things we don't mean."

"Maybe we should! Maybe we need to have this out. Tell me, Shekinah. Tell me how you feel."

"I feel hurt. And angry. But I'm not going to let you push me into regretting my words. You're out of balance, Alejandro. Ask your witches for a reading, or to kick your ass across the astral plane, or whatever else you need. I'm not going to do it for you."

She walked across the living room, grabbed her boots and purse, and headed toward the vestibule and the front door.

"I'll see you at Raquel's tonight. We still have to deal with Tish. She needs our help." Her voice caught when she said that. Betraying her.

"Shekinah..."

Turning at the door, she looked at the man she loved and saw the confusion there. If what she'd already said didn't make him understand, she didn't have the words. Maybe they'd get to the words someday, but not right now.

"Alejandro...I'm the one that needs a little space right now. We can talk more tonight. Before or after we meet with Tish is up to you. But I have too much work on my plate to spend all afternoon hashing this out."

"Okay," he said, voice hard again.

"Okay," she replied, opened the door, and shut it behind her.

She padded down the stairs in her socks, boots in hand, and cried.

15

ALEJANDRO

Well, fuck.

Alejandro stood, staring at the closed front door. What, exactly, had just happened?

You know, doofus.

So the real question was, how in the world had he *let* that happen? She was right. He'd been trying to pick a fight. To get her to rip one of his scabs off so he could attack. Blame her, even. And fighting that way? She was right. It wasn't how they did things. Some of their arguments over the past five years had hurt, sure, but they'd never been purposefully hurtful. Right now he felt like one of those guys that picked fights in bars just to feel the power of getting punched in the face and being able to punch back.

Was his life so hard that he needed to fight some unseen force about it?

No. It wasn't. He was a privileged pendejo, whose life was damn sweet.

Disgust roiling in his belly, Alejandro walked back to the common room, dumped the cups of tea in the sink, and placed the mugs into the dishwasher. Then he realized what he was doing. What he always tried to do.

Restoring order. Setting things in place. Tidying up so he didn't have to look at the mess. Ever. Except, *he* was a fucking mess. Maybe he should just give up, answer some of those emails piling up, desperate for his services. Take on some paying work. Pretend his life was righteous and exactly the way he wanted it.

Except he couldn't. He couldn't work for the polluters and exploiters anymore. Couldn't make their machines hum more efficiently for the sole purpose of making them more money. He'd held that knowledge in abeyance for as long as could could; now, it tore at his soul. He felt...frayed. Angry. Tired.

"Damn it."

From the kitchen counter and the coffee table, his ancestors smirked at him.

::You think life is tidy, mijo? You have a lot to learn.::

Yeah, well.

Alejandro sighed. He'd been doing a lot of that lately. Damn it. He'd really looked forward to seeing Shekinah. And the night with Thomas had been...nice. He hadn't felt that alive, or that sexy, in quite a while.

And how do you think Shekinah feels?

He just never thought of it. She was always so sexy to him. A gorgeous woman with a huge heart and even bigger smile. He'd always loved that her spiritual practice was even stronger than his. Loved her confidence.

And when was the last time you told her any of this?

He just figured she knew. After five years, it didn't seem like he had to say it anymore. But maybe that was part of the problem. He counted on the relationship but hadn't pulled his weight for a while, even before things in his life went south.

The base of his skull pinged again, and he scanned the room. The photos and family objects...but no. It was the big, colorful weaving again, with the upraised arms and red bands of color. And then there was the smaller one next to it, that he hadn't really paid attention to in the early morning light. That one was all done in shades of black, white, and gray. As he approached the weavings, it felt almost as if there was a force field around them. Had there always been? Was that another thing he just hadn't noticed?

No. This was different. Something new.

::*Because it is time.*:: the ancestors said. ::*Time that you learn.*::

Learn what, though? Great Gods and Goddesses, he hoped this wasn't some damn midlife initiation process. He'd been through enough initiatory rites with the coven.

Then, one corner of the black and gray weaving caught his eye. A tiny leaf shape, gone unnoticed. Then another, in the opposite corner. His eye searched all four corners, picking out the small, black objects, pictures, woven into the larger pattern so seamlessly...they looked like spear tips, or leaf blades.

::!::

The base of his skull flared.

"What?"

::*Pay attention.*::

He stared at the weaving. *Show me more,* he thought. What did the symbols mean? Nothing. No response. Just the same weavings that had hung on his wall for years, ever since his abuelo had gifted him with them, the first one upon high school graduation, the second, after he graduated college and got his first client.

He tried to open the energy centers at the soles of his feet, and in the palms of hands. Tried to deepen his breathing. But he was too off kilter. Out of balance.

Out of practice. The disruption of routine had toppled all of his practices. Raquel and Brenda would tell him it was time to get back to it all, and he would. But first, the ancestors needed their ofrenda.

That, he could build.

16

SHEKINAH

aquel's home was a beautiful old Craftsman with gleaming wood and good bones, but what made it special was the way Raquel had made the place a home. A big red sofa faced a fireplace, comfy-looking chairs and ottomans, and a bright painting of a small Black boy, face alight with joy, arms upraised to the sun.

"That's a portrait of Zion when he was around five. It's the Tarot card, The Sun."

Raquel set down a tray with a squat brown teapot and four mismatched cups.

"It's beautiful." Zion had greeted Shekinah when she arrived. She really liked the boy. "It's funny, all these years, and I've never spent time in your living room. I think I've only been over for garden parties in the summer."

"Yeah. Alejandro is here all the time for coven meetings, but we don't really socialize much outside of coven."

Raquel plopped down on the other end of the couch, and tucked one jean clad leg under the other. Shekinah had always admired Raquel. Brenda, too. From what Alejandro had told her, it seemed like the two women led the coven with light and graceful hands, but weren't afraid to throw down if necessary.

"Alejandro's giving you trouble, isn't he?"

Shekinah sighed, and wished she already had a mug in her hands. It would give her something to do besides look around at the art on the walls and avoid this woman's gaze. Her eyes were almost as penetrating as Shekinah's teacher's.

"I'm not sure what to do, Raquel. I love him. We love each other. But he's being such a shit lately. He tried to pick a fight with me today."

Finally, Raquel leaned forward and poured steaming, fragrant tea into the two mugs. "What about?"

"Well, too much information, but...our sex life has been almost nonexistent lately, and I've been giving him his space. You know. To work things out. But he picked someone up last night, brought them to his home, and had sex. I'd gone over all prepared to have a relationship conversation, and was confronted with that. That's when he deflected. Tried to pick a fight."

She blew across the surface of the tea. Some sort of spiced blend.

"That's low."

"Right?"

"He's flailing, and I know you know that. Brenda and I are definitely going to be kicking his ass if he doesn't start finding a way through soon. We've been hoping he'd figure it out on his own before it came to that."

The tea tasted faintly of apples, cardamom, and cinnamon. It was comforting, almost as if the witch knew she needed it. It smelled like October.

"Thanks for letting me come early. It helps to know I'm not overreacting to all of this."

Raquel tucked her other leg up, folding her curvy frame cross legged on the sofa.

"I'm happy to help if I can. We try to not interfere in coven members' lives too much, but it's pretty clear to me that you and Alejandro are good for one another, and that he's gonna need more support moving forward. You're part of his support system, so…"

"So I get some support, too."

Raquel smiled. "Something like that. And I know you've got your own practice, but if you ever need a reading, or help with a spiritual cleansing for your person or your space, just let Brenda or me know. And before you ask, Alejandro knows I was going to make the offer."

Shekinah settled back into the sofa. "That's actually a relief. I don't want to be going behind his back to the people he relies on. That's not how our relationship works. Although right now? I'm not sure how it works at all."

"Give it time. My sense is that he's on the cusp of something. He'll break through soon."

"You think so?"

"He always does."

There was a knock at the door, and Raquel set down her mug and rose to answer. She heard Raquel greet whoever was there. Heard the rustling of a coat. A woman's voice.

Tish.

Was it bad that she felt relieved? Alejandro would be here soon, but the longer she could avoid it…

Shekinah set her own mug down and stood to greet her friend. She looked even worse than last time, with purple shadows beneath her eyes.

"Tish."

"Oh. Shekinah."

Shekinah embraced her friend, who tucked her head against her shoulder.

"Have you had more visions?"

"Yes. And they're bad. Really, really bad."

What could be worse than seeing your brother shot on the sidewalk? Shekinah didn't want to imagine.

"Sit. Have a cup of tea. Tell us about it," Raquel said, directing Tish to one of the comfy-looking chairs that flanked the fireplace.

"Did Shekinah..."

"Yes. I know about the vision of your brother. Can you tell us about the others?"

Raquel leaned forward to pour tea.

Tish began to shake, violently. Raquel rose and crouched at her side, one hand on Tish's knee, the other on her arm.

"Sister? Take a breath for me, okay?"

Shekinah watched as Tish struggled, one hand clutching the chair arm so hard it looked as though her fingers might snap.

"Breathe in deep. All the way down to just above your pubic bone. That's right. Slow it down."

In moments, Raquel had a woman on the verge of a panic attack breathing almost normally. Impressive.

"Okay. I'm going to stay right here. Tell us what you need to."

Tish nodded, then looked directly at Shekinah with those exhausted eyes.

"This is so much...I can't say it's worse. But it's so bad! Terrifying. I can't... It's..."

"Keep breathing," Raquel said, voice warm and completely calm. Shekinah realized she was holding her own breath, and exhaled, then drew a measured breath in through her nose.

Tish fumbled in her pants pocket and came out with a tissue. Blew her nose.

"I'm okay. I'm okay. Thanks."

Raquel backed off and gave her some space, but Shekinah noticed she sat in the chair across from Tish rather than moving back to the couch.

"Look, we all know about the police. Targeting people. After I saw you yesterday morning I'd half convinced myself it was just my fears for my brother, showing up in my subconscious. That's natural, right?"

Shekinah nodded. "Makes sense."

Tish continued, looking over Shekinah's head now, as if watching a scene on the wall. "But I swear, what I'm seeing is so much worse than that. It scares me so bad."

Worse than your brother getting killed? This didn't even make sense.

"It's like…"

"It's like what?" Shekinah leaned forward, elbow on her knees, peering at her friend. She could feel the air in the room changing. Becoming thicker. Heavier. It was as if someone were pumping steam into the room.

"It's like…I swear, they're doing something. Something bad. I saw flashes. Images. Stars. Metal. Fire. People in robes. Some sort of…"

Raquel swore under her breath, then said a word Shekinah couldn't catch.

"What did you just say, Raquel?"

"Magic. It sounds like you're seeing scenes of people doing magic."

"Not just people. The police." Tish's eyes were wide with fear. "I saw the police doing those things. I swear."

17

ALEJANDRO

"How did you know it was the police?" Alejandro asked. He had focused his attention on Tish to avoid the pain and anger in Shekinah's eyes. Goddesses, he knew he'd fucked up, but trouble was, he had no idea how to fix it. He didn't know how to fix one damn thing.

So. He'd concentrate on seeing if the coven could help Shekinah's friend. Maybe that would be one step toward reconciling. Yeah, he really hated messes. And he hated hurting Shekinah even more.

"Well, there were the stars. Like metal badges. Six-pointed. Five-pointed. But not the ones you guys wear."

"Not a classic pentacle," Raquel said.

"Right. Filled in. Solid. Like a cop's shield. Plus, there was something about how they moved." She looked at Alejandro then, and in her anger, he saw a flash of the woman she usually was, bright, with a luminosity and strength that was different than Shekinah's, but there all the same. He saw why they were friends. "You know how cops move. You, too."

She turned to Raquel at that. Both Alejandro and Raquel nodded their heads.

"It's that swagger they all have. As if they're gunslingers in the Wild West."

Alejandro gasped. All three women snapped their heads toward him.

"Stay with it," Raquel said. "Don't push it away."

Right. Good. She knew something was happening. He was going to be okay. A slight tingle of discomfort at doing this in front of Tish and Shekinah and then... He was going to be okay.

And he was surrounded by flames. And in front of him was a cross, burning. And all around him were shields on fire. Stars. There were stars everywhere. And horses screaming. Gunfire. Laughter. The feel of rope around his waist and wrists. A jerk. And he was being dragged.

"What's happening to him?"

Panic. He jerked and rolled. Slammed against hard earth again.

"Ssh. He'll be fine."

Then louder, near his ear? "You're okay, Alejandro. We're right here." A soothing, familiar voice.

Choking. Dust filled mouth and nose. Couldn't breathe. Couldn't see. Body bashed and scraped. Over and over and over. Bones cracking. Skin flayed open. And it would. Not. Stop. The bumping, dragging speed of it. Sound of hooves.

And that laughter again. And finally, one last image of a star, shining in his eyes. Then. Nothing.

Alejandro seized up, then choked, coughing, gasping for air. Eyes fluttering. Ice pick of a headache lancing his brain. Blinked.

"Too bright."

"Turn the overhead lights off." Raquel's voice. Raquel.

He was sitting on Raquel's red couch in her living room. There wasn't any fire. His body wasn't being dragged behind...

"Horses." He struggled to sit up. When had he lain down? Gods, his body hurt, and not like he'd been to the gym. He coughed again, trying to clear the nonexistent dust from his throat.

"Here. The tea should be cool enough to just drink down. Swallow that, and we'll get you some water. And maybe some ibuprofen, from the looks of things. Those are in the cabinet next to the fridge." That last wasn't spoken to him.

He half saw Raquel gesture to Shekinah, who headed through the swinging door to the kitchen. Shekinah. She was still here. He felt a rush of relief.

"I thought I was alone."

She came back with a clear tumbler of water, other hand cupped around the pills. Crouching next to the couch, she offered both. Raquel took the tea mug from his hands. As he reached for the tumbler, he wrapped his fingers around his lover's hand. His lover. Still. After all his shit. There she was...

"You're not alone, Alejandro. I'm right here. So is Raquel. We see you. We know you."

He began to weep. Big, rolling sobs that hunched him forward. Heard the thunk of glass on table, and then her arms were around him. Holding him.

"You are precious to me, Alejandro. I don't know what's going on with you, but whatever it is, we'll get through this. Just stick with me, kid. We're going places."

Through his sobs, he gasped out a small laugh, then folded more deeply into her body, allowing her strength to hold him up. Just for a minute. Just for now.

"I'm sorry," he said through the tears and the phlegm.

"I know. Ssshhh. It's okay. We'll be okay."

He hoped that it was true. But for now, it felt good to hear the words, and to feel her, and to smell the warm incense scent that permeated her hair.

Finally, his breathing slowed. He shifted back, away from his lover's body. She allowed her arms to slide down his, giving him space, but not letting him go.

"I need a tissue. Got one?"

Raquel left the room and returned with a box. After wiping his face and blowing his nose, he reached for the water glass and ibuprofen on the coffee table. Shekinah curled up on the couch beside him, hand on his thigh.

"It seems like your visions are as bad as mine," Tish said. "Shit. I'm kind of glad someone else is seeing something, gotta admit."

"I'm sympathetic but...damn. We called you here mostly to see if we could help you control your visions, give you some psychic tech. I didn't expect to get pulled into visions of my own." He looked at Raquel. "Sorry, boss. I've been slacking on my practice."

She grimaced, then picked up the teapot and headed back toward kitchen.

"I'll let it go this time." She paused at the swinging door and looked back at him, face grown serious again. "But clearly you need more help than we've been giving you, and I'm sorry about that. It's back to daily practice for you, and psychic basics, and weekly check-ins with Brenda or me, and all the rest of it."

"Message received."

She walked through the swinging door.

In truth, he felt relieved that he wasn't trying to hide it anymore. He was a wreck, and the people he trusted still loved him. He leaned into Shekinah, who shifted her arm from his leg to around his shoulders, pulling him closer.

"Once Raquel gets back with more tea, you're going to have to tell us more about what you saw."

"I know." Just thinking about talking about it brought the sense of choking dust back into his throat and nose. He cleared his throat and took a drink of water, then blew his nose again.

"And Tish?" she said. "The coven really can help you. I know it. They have all sorts of energy techniques that should help. Right, Alejandro?"

He cleared his throat again. "We do. And we can start on those today. Someone with your spiritual training has a leg up on someone coming in fresh, so that's good. You'll probably find most of the techniques familiar, at least in essence. What Raquel will help you do is get better focus on this specific thing: dealing with unbidden visions."

Raquel was back then, teapot wrapped in a towel.

"I heard that last part, and he's right. It all starts with breath and energy flow, which I hear you kundalini people are good at." She smiled, placed the pot back on the tray and sat back down. "Alejandro, you said something about horses."

Oh Gods. "It was really bad. I was being dragged. Tied up. Shit. And there was fire."

Shekinah squeezed his shoulder. "Oh, love."

He looked at Tish then, who sat, preternaturally still, eyes trained on him.

"And I saw stars. A sheriff's badge."

Tish opened her mouth, then closed it again.

"Do you know who you were? Because this vision feels different than Tish's. Tish's was a possible future, right?" Raquel asked.

Tish nodded. "I think so. But it felt so real. It felt like it had already happened."

"But it hasn't. So, premonition."

Face shocked, Tish started to reply. Raquel held up a hand to stall her. "I'll get back to that. Don't freak out yet."

His coven mentor turned her wise, dark eyes back on him. "But your vision? The way you describe it, it sounds as if it was sometime in the past. So I'll ask it again, any idea who you were?"

One image from the scene snapped into clear focus, quickly overlaid by the image of hands, weaving yarn into rugs. The base of his skull started buzzing so loud, he could barely hear himself think.

"Yes. I do. I was my however-many-greats grand uncle. Alejandro Juan. I'm named for him and my abuelo, Guillermo."

"What happened?" Shekinah asked, voice soft. "Do you know his story?"

Throat tightening, nose tingling. There came the tears again. He swallowed, hard. If he didn't keep the tears at bay, he'd never get through this.

"Most Mexicans in Oregon worked on the railroads, or as miners. Some were mule packers for the Army, which isn't something to be proud of, considering they were fighting the indigenous people here, and most Mexicans are at least part, if not all, indigenous." He shrugged.

"Not agriculture?" Shekinah asked.

"That came later. My family arrived a lot earlier than most, this far north, working as vaqueros for a Spaniard. Late 1700s. Four generations in, they'd been able to save enough money to have their *own* cattle. They became pretty prosperous, actually, with a family ranchero, around sixty miles from here. Then some white men decided a bunch of dumb vaqueros couldn't have built that up honestly."

"So they accused your family of stealing." Raquel's voice was flat.

Alejandro nodded. "Yeah. They couldn't get to my uncle's father. He was too powerful by that time."

"So they targeted his son," Tish said. "Those bastards."

"They killed him. Tied him up. Beat him. Then dragged him behind horses until he was dead."

"Oh my God. Love. I'm so sorry." Shekinah's warmth broke through his fragile shell.

He let the tears come again. For himself. For all of his ancestors.

And mostly, for Alejandro Juan.

18

SHEKINAH

Shekinah parked at a distance from the Shiva Center because she wanted a chance to walk. Gather herself. She liked walking beneath the trees with their turning leaves, and past the rock garden on the corner, and the mix of Craftsman and Victorian homes. This end of the street was peaceful. Quiet. As though it lived to balance out the more commercial stretch not so far down the road. As she walked from streetlight puddle to streetlight puddle, she tried to match her breathing with her steps. One inhalation for every four boot strikes. The cadence of walking helped, and the scent of night blooming jasmine soothed her soul.

On one hand, she was more worried about Alejandro than ever. On the other, she was relieved that he'd had some sort of a breakthrough. It was hell not being with him, but she had her appointment with Yogi Basu and he needed to meet with his coven.

They had promised one another that they would spend the night together, the way both their calendars said they would. Whether you lived together or not, it was the little commitments that seemed to make or break a relationship.

Sometimes the big commitments were easy, assumed. The little ones became easy to skip, ignore, or let slide over time. So tonight, their bodies would lie side by side. They would breathe the same air, as they drifted off to sleep.

Maybe they'd even have sex, though she still wasn't counting on it, not after all of today's bruises. But you never knew. Sometimes the deeper the anguish, the hotter the sex. She smiled. Yeah, having sex with Alejandro tonight would be really great. She'd see what she could do to make that happen.

Her feet led her to the Center, just as they always did. Her other heart home. She felt a clenching in her chest, and paused, just staring up the short walkway to the three steps, and the dark wood door. A massive Craftsman with solid pillars, it stood, lights glowing warmly, like a refuge in the night.

"Ravana ordered his chariot fetched. Surrounded by his warriors, he drove into battle in the golden ratha." She recited the words from the great epic, the Ramayana, into the evening air, not sure whether she actually believed them. But sometimes you had to act as if, right? She could pretend she had a chariot and could call up the strength of a child of Shiva into herself. At least a little bit.

"Here goes." She stepped onto the path, walked up the three steps, and opened the big wooden door. The building was quiet, class having let out half an hour or so before. A couple of students sat chatting on chairs in the small reception room to the right. She shucked her boots by the door, gave them a wave and continued down the hallway lined with warm wood wainscoting, past all the framed photos of great teachers hung above. And then, all that was left was a three-panel wood door, standing slightly ajar.

Shekinah knocked.

"Come in," said Yogi Basu.

She wiped her hands on her jeans, pushed the door open and walked into his office. Immediately, she felt a palpable sense of peace. As if all her fears were for nothing, and she could finally relax. Her feet padded across the rich carpet, woven in threads of navy and red, not looking at the floor-to-ceiling bookcases she'd seen a thousand times. Barely noticing the pots of orchids by the window. Seeing only him, sitting behind a big oak desk, surrounded by books and papers, smiling at her. Luminous, eyes glowing as warmly as the brass lamp on his desktop. His thinning hair was neat as usual, though his beard needed combing.

She paused three feet from the desk, put her hands together and gave a slight bow. "Good evening, Yogi Basu."

"Sit down, Shekinah. Know that you are welcome here."

That. That was what she so longed to hear. Tears pricked at the edges of her eyes. She looked down as she sat, hiding her response.

"You never need to hide emotion from me. Emotions are our teachers, just as everything in life can teach. Sometimes emotions are the strongest teachers of all, if we do not let them control us. Yes?"

"Yes."

He steepled his hands on the desk and leaned forward slightly, desk chair creaking beneath his weight.

"So. What have you come to talk with me about?"

"Teacher training, and..." She paused.

"Initiation."

She mashed her lips together and lightly bit the folded flesh. As soon as she caught herself, Shekinah released her lips from between her teeth. An old habit from her teenage years; she didn't do that anymore.

"What seems to be the issue?"

"I'm polyamorous."

If it was possible, Yogi Basu smiled even more broadly than before. "You love many people? So do I! I love every person that walks through that front door." He gestured toward the front of the house, as if they could see the door. As if they weren't sequestered in his safe womb of an office. "I don't *like* all of them, mind you. But love? That is our task in this world. To love. To become light. Yes?"

Shoving down the fluttering in her belly, Shekinah inhaled as slowly and deeply as she could. She was going to have to be careful. Find the right words.

"It isn't that. I mean, of course it is. But it isn't *just* that. I have a partner, Alejandro. We love each other. I also have a girlfriend, Maureen. I've been with Alejandro for five years and with Maureen for two."

"And they both know this?'

"Of course!" He shocked the words out of her.

He nodded thoughtfully, then sat in silence, looking toward one of the tall bookcases. She folded her hands in her lap and trained her eyes on the large image of Lord Shiva on the wall above Yogi Basu's desk. His right palm faced outward, in the Abhaya mudrā, representing fearlessness, and the promise of protection. She needed both.

"It is not my way. But that does not mean it is impossible. If you practice truth with your partners as you say?" He paused.

She nodded.

"And you feel that living in this way supports your dharma?"

She nodded again.

"As long as you are in your integrity, and loving in this way strengthens you, anything is possible."

Her breath left her chest in a whoosh.

"Really?"

He pursed his lips, frowning slightly. "I probe my heart and find that it does not offend me, this kind of love you speak of." He looked at her and smiled. Not a big smile, but a smile, nonetheless. She'd take it.

"I have heard of such things, of course, as one does, but have never met anyone who practiced in this way."

Shekinah sat, stunned. Out of words, and suddenly exhausted. It had been a very, very long day.

"So, we have addressed your troubles?"

"Most of them."

"There are others?"

She looked into her own heart and found that her other worries seemed to have faded, at least for the moment.

"Not right now. No."

He waved a hand as if to say, *Well, all right, then.*

She nodded and began to rise.

"Shekinah?"

She stopped, halfway between sitting and standing, and decided to stand the rest of the way.

"You pray every day?"

"Yes, Yogi."

"That is good. Be well. I shall see you next time."

She pressed her palms together and gave a slight bow to him, and to the portrait of Shiva behind his desk.

"Thank you, teacher."

She left, head still filled with questions, but with a heart much lighter than when she had arrived.

19

ALEJANDRO

Alejandro loaded the dishwasher in Raquel's kitchen, cleaning up with Zion as Raquel greeted the members of Arrow and Crescent coven who'd started trickling in.

After the intensity of his visions, and the emotional aftermath, he'd just wanted to go home and curl up into a ball, but Raquel had convinced him to stay for dinner and the coven meeting. She'd insisted that not only did Tish need their help, but he did, too. So, the already scheduled meeting was going ahead, even if it had a different agenda than just last-minute pre-Samhain planning.

He swore, the past year had messed up so many Sabbats, he might as well count them twelve for twelve. Only a few of the solar feast days had been celebrated unscathed by local politics or some magical crisis or another. Good thing Arrow and Crescent was well trained enough to roll with the punches.

"I think that's it," Alejandro said, looking around the kitchen and the round table in the dining area as Zion put the last of the leftover eggplant lasagna into the big stainless fridge.

"Yep. Think so," Zion replied. He was thirteen now, and seemed equally proud of his raggedy Afro and his Captain America T-shirt. "Guess I'll head to my room."

"See you, Zion."

Alejandro grabbed a sponge and wiped down the marble countertops. Alejandro appreciated a tidy kitchen, and Raquel did, too. She might a single parent with a full time job running her own café but that didn't mean she let things slide at home. The opposite was true, in fact.

But even she tells you to loosen up sometimes. And that the fact that you're so anal has made this rough patch even harder.

He had no in between, it seemed. Only total structure or feeling as if the world was falling apart. He sighed. Well, he was going to work on that, wasn't he?

Selene poked their head through the kitchen door, then entered. "We're all here. Lucy and Tobias just arrived." Dressed all in black as usual, their long black hair a sheet around their pale face, Selene looked concerned. "You okay? You kind of look like hell, which is unusual for you."

"Thanks for the compliment. I don't know if I'm okay. But you'll hear all about it in a minute. I don't want to tell the story more than once."

"Fair enough. Raquel also sent me in to get fizzy water and a bottle of Pinot."

He raised his eyebrows at that. The coven used to never drink at meetings, never did more than share a libation at the end of ritual, in fact. But this past year had taken a toll on everyone. Once the tide turned, they were going to have to discuss it, Brenda had said, but for now, he guessed Raquel figured some folks at least were going to want a glass of wine.

"I'll get the glasses if you grab the wine," he said.

Soon enough, they were settled in the living room with the other coven members. Lucky number nine. Three times three. Alejandro went for the fizzy water. After the afternoon he'd had, the last thing he needed was alcohol.

"What do we need to know?" Lucy asked. Always direct, and ready to go, Lucy helped sheep dog the meetings when they got too far off track. "I've got an early start in the morning and can't stay past eleven."

Alejandro looked around the room, scanning the faces of the people who'd become like family to him over the years, even the newer members, like Cassiel, Moss, and Tobias, sitting together on the couch. A riot of red curls. Black hair in a fauxhawk. Brown hair and goatee. Shit. They looked young to him, too. Was that insulting, and part of his crisis, or just real? They were witches, just like him, and had skills he didn't have. Everyone in the coven was trained in magical and psychic basics, but each of them had a specialty, too.

Tempest, a healer, was looking kind of fragile. Her short, platinum-blond hair—previously dyed any variety of unnatural colors—only made her face look even paler than before. He had heard whispers that she struggled with chronic illness, but so far, she hadn't come out to the whole coven...At any rate, no time to worry about that right now. Tempest and Lucy sat on chairs filched from the dining room. Lucy wore spattered painter's pants, her dark brown hair caught back in a ponytail. Selene sat next to him, both of them on overstuffed cushions, cross-legged on the floor. Brenda and Raquel, their high priestesses and mentors, sat in the two chairs flanking the cold fireplace. Pretty soon, it would be cold enough outside to light the fire.

He realized they were all waiting for him to start.

"Sorry," he said. "I'm not sure where to begin, because there are at least three things to discuss tonight, so I'll just dive in and hope you can figure it out."

"That's what we're here for," Tobias quipped, running his fingers over his goatee.

Alejandro ignored his coven brother. Now that it was time to talk, his stomach wasn't too happy with the eggplant parmesan. Considering his career success was based mostly on his ability to explain things to people without making them feel ignorant, rather than his stellar IT skills, this nervousness was a new sensation. He didn't like it. *Okay. Just dive in.*

"Shekinah's friend Tish started having visions, including one in which she saw her brother shot dead on a sidewalk."

"Damn," Moss said. "That's messed up."

"Then my ancestors started pinging me, and I figured, 'tis the season, right? So I got a new ofrenda console, got out the old photos...and things got worse. They're also trying to show me something in these two woven rugs I have. They showed me symbols that I never noticed before. I brought pictures."

"You have to tell them, Alejandro," Raquel said, gesturing with her glass of red wine. "The only way out is through."

Alejandro closed his eyes for a moment, sending a quick prayer to his ancestors for help. For guidance. His throat began to close again. He cleared it, sipped more fizzy water, and began.

"Today I had a vision of one of my ancestors being dragged until dead by a bunch of white men, including a sheriff."

"Alejandro!" Selene grabbed his hand. He jerked away

and shook his head. If he was going to get through this without breaking down, he couldn't handle sympathy.

"I heard horses. Felt myself being dragged. And then I saw firelight, reflected off a badge. A star."

"And Tish saw stars, too," Raquel said. "Five- and six-pointed. And she said they weren't the kind we wear."

"What the hell?" Lucy said. "What in Tonantzin's name are we looking at here?"

"That's what we need to figure out." Brenda finally spoke from her chair. Her eyes were closed and she fingered the enormous moonstone that always rested on her chest. "There are threads from the past. Threads from a possible future. Both are connected by the power of these stars."

"And by violence," Raquel reminded her.

"And by violence," Brenda echoed. "And family. Lineage. Blood."

She opened her eyes and stared at Alejandro. He could tell she was in some liminal space, not really seeing him, or seeing around him. Neither here nor there. "You said there were weavings. Show them."

He pulled out his laptop, where he'd stored photos from his phone. Each member of the coven looked at one, and then the other. No one spoke. He could hear Zion, talking to someone on the phone in his room. A car driving by outside. Finally, the computer reached Brenda. She looked at it with those half-hooded eyes.

"Attack and protection. Protection, and attack. We must be prepared for both, on every front. There are more innocent lives at stake, and a frightening power that once again stalks the land. It was seeded long ago, back as far as your ancestor's arrival, Alejandro. And it works among us today."

Brenda took in a shuddering breath, blinked her blue

eyes, and released the moonstone. She rolled her head and shrugged her shoulders, then shook out her hands.

"That's all my spirit allies gave me," she said.

"So what is this about? Who or what are we defending from or preparing to attack?" Tempest's voice was quiet, but asked the question Alejandro didn't really want the answer to.

Lucy snorted. "Not to be rude, but isn't it obvious?"

She looked from Moss, to Alejandro, to Selene, to Raquel. All of the most marginalized people in the coven. Each of them nodded. Alejandro found himself nodding, too, the answer crowding at the back of his head.

"It's the cops," Moss finally said. "Damn it."

Damn it, indeed. Alejandro was not ready for this one. He wasn't even certain how to be.

20

SHEKINAH

Alejandro fumbled his keys from the pocket of his slacks. It was funny to see him in a rumpled shirt, not starched and perfect. Funny, and a little heartbreaking, too. Shekinah knew what today had cost him.

Opening the door, he let her pass. She went straight through to the big common space and dumped her purse on the long, golden-brown leather couch. Then she saw it, a brand new mid-twentieth-century piece, a console filled with photographs, marigolds in small, brightly painted vases, and some traditional Mexican art. The new console was gorgeous, like all of his pieces were, which gave her a minor pang. What would they do with their furniture if they ever ended up wanting to move in together? What sort of home would they settle on?

"I like the new altar."

"The ancestors insisted," he said, coming to stand next to her. "I've been neglecting them and they weren't very happy about it."

She felt his fingers on hers, soft, tapping at her fingertips, asking the question. She opened her fingers and laced his hand into her own. The answer. For now, at least.

"I know they're not the only thing I've been neglecting. I'm so sorry, Shekinah. Sorry about everything."

She turned to look at him. Her partner. Her lover. Her friend. The witch who, the first time they met, looked at her with eyes that swore they *saw* her. Knew her.

"Do you think you're going to be okay?" And yet another question, beneath the spoken one: Are *we* going to be okay?

He gave her a gentle kiss, then rested his forehead against hers. "I think so. I want to be now, so that's something."

"You didn't want to be okay?"

"I think I liked flailing a little bit. I...got sick of having everything in my life together all the time, maybe. Don't get me wrong, I'm still fucked up, and can't make any promises yet, but I'm ready to start trying again. Get back in the saddle."

As soon as the words left his mouth, his face changed, crumbling back in on itself.

"Oh, Alejandro." She folded him in her arms, breathing in the scent of his skin. "I'm so sorry about your uncle. This has to be hard. Want to sit and talk about it some more?"

She felt him shake his head.

"No," he murmured. "Not tonight. What I want more than anything right now is to take you to my bed. I want to make love to you tonight, Shekinah, if that's all right with you. And after that? I want to eat ice cream and ask how your meeting with your teacher went."

She released the breath she didn't even know she'd been holding. Turning her head, she kissed his perfect brown ear.

"I want that, too," she whispered. Pulling away from him,

she caught his hand again and led him to his perfect bedroom, where she hoped to make messy, sloppy love.

21

ALEJANDRO

The sun was out, but there was a definite chill to the air. Alejandro walked next to Brenda on the tree-lined streets around Hawthorne Boulevard. Tempest was watching the Inner Eye, Brenda's shop, and it was slow enough that Brenda had agreed to a break and a walk. So here they were, both in light coats against the autumn chill, her boots and his shoes making a syncopated rhythm on the sidewalk. Slowing his long stride to match hers, he avoided fallen chestnuts that looked like a Tribble colony on the sidewalk.

While half of him appreciated the maples that shaded from orange and yellow, to the deep red of the Japanese variety, he was also half lost in himself, barely paying attention to the blue car about to turn until Brenda laid a hand on his coat sleeve, stopping him from crossing the street.

Being around his priestess was soothing, comforting to the confused boy inside of him. She'd asked about his practice and he was doing his best to answer as they walked. Walking was good, too. His body craved movement, he realized. Not working meant he wasn't walking to client meetings downtown, and he hadn't bothered with the gym in three months.

At some point between the horrible visions in Raquel's living room, the sweet, half-sad sex with Shekinah, and talking over ice cream afterward, Alejandro decided he needed to recommit. To his practice and to Shekinah, and he supposed he could add his body back in there, too. There were still other questions in the air, and he was probably going to need to see a therapist, or start dosing with CBD, but every person had to start somewhere, right?

So before heading out to meet with Brenda, he had spent ten minutes on his meditation cushion, just breathing, letting the jumble of thoughts and emotions do their thing. Then he poured fresh cups of water for the ancestors on the ofrenda, and spent some time listening. They hadn't wanted to talk, but he'd gotten a sense that they were happy with the new altar space, at least.

"That's a start," Brenda was saying, flipping the collar of her gray coat up. "A good one, actually. Congratulations, Alejandro."

He chuffed out a small laugh. "Congratulations? Thanks, boss. But frankly? I feel ashamed. Ashamed that my life feels like a mess, that I've hurt Shekinah, and let the coven down."

Brenda stopped suddenly and whipped toward him. Startled, he felt his foot rock on top of a spiny chestnut and barely saved his ankle from turning.

"Let the coven down? What in the world are you talking about?"

He threw his hands in the air. "I'm a wreck, Brenda! A forty-five-year-old wreck! I'm supposed to be there for the rest of the coven. And I almost seriously messed things up last month."

She started walking again. He paused, then fell back into step.

"You think you messed things up?"

"Yes, with GranCo. I could've..."

"Could've what, exactly? As soon as you found out what they were doing, you quit the project. And you helped the coven, despite your NDA."

He was silent, hands clenched, resisting the urge to kick the Goddess-damned Tribbles out of the way with his pointy shoes.

"Right?" she prodded.

He just walked, mind darting with half-thoughts, not able to see a clear path. Not able to make the connections he needed to make.

"It doesn't feel like enough," he finally ground out. "And, things with Shekinah are a little bit better after yesterday, but that's not good enough, either. I'm still lost, Brenda. And I hate feeling this way."

"No one likes feeling lost, Alejandro, especially not control freaks like us."

He stopped again, aghast. "You?"

It was her turn to laugh, though her laughter had more humor in it than his had. "Why do you think I own my own business? And run my own coven? And how do you think I got the courage to get Carolyn away from her abusive bastard of a husband? Your problem is that you still think your so-called flaws aren't also your strengths. It's time you face those demons, Alejandro."

"I did my demon work..."

"Before your second-degree initiation. I know. You think that's where it stops? You think there isn't round upon round of inner work we need to do? What exactly do you think you're going through now?"

"But I integrated those demons."

"You established a better relationship with them," she corrected. "This round? You need to really ask them what they need, and start giving it to them. It's time, Alejandro. Time for your demons to become the allies they really want to be."

"But..."

"What got you through your childhood, Alejandro? What helped you deal with the bullies, and figure out maybe it was okay to be bisexual? What helps you give Catarina's kids the stability they need?"

"I don't know! I just...did it. Do it. I just do things!"

"That isn't true, and you know it."

They had circled around the block and were back on the busy street again, walking past shops and restaurants, walking past people pushing strollers and holding cups of coffee. Life. The trees were life. The sidewalks were life. The people were life.

"I don't know what I know right now," he said.

Brenda stopped in front of the Inner Eye. Crystals winked behind her, catching the sun.

"I know," she replied. "But you will."

She took both of his hands in hers and pierced him with those damn psychic blue eyes that saw way too much of everything. He couldn't escape those eyes, or Raquel's either. And that's why they were still his teachers.

"Keep going with your practice, and you'll be fine. You'll see. And listen to your ancestors. They're not done with you, yet. These visions of yours and Tish's aren't done."

That was exactly what he was afraid of. It was also one of the reasons he had become a witch.

To listen. To see visions. To help do something on this earth besides work for a living and make other people rich.

22

SHEKINAH

The sidewalk was crammed with angry people, spilling out onto the street next to a small, hedge-bordered open parking lot. Shekinah supposed it was a small crowd, as crowds went, maybe fifty people all told, but for a weekday morning impromptu gathering, that seemed like a lot.

She'd never been to a gathering like this, so had no real gauge for protest crowds. She never participated when Alejandro went out, figuring everyone had their work to do in this world, and being out in the streets just wasn't hers. Protests weren't really her thing. Activism was for other people, she thought. Her work was to donate money to various causes when she had it, and to try to raise her own vibration, to cause less harm in this pain-filled world.

And to take care of Alejandro when and if he needed it, during the times when things got intense.

The crowd was comprised of a lot of young people—Black, brown, and white—with some middle-aged white activist types that ringed the edges, and a few Black elders in a clump near the hedge, supporting a weeping man.

Dispersed throughout the group were people with hand-made cardboard signs they held aloft, reading *Justice for Jeremy* and *PPB is Guilty*

"They killed my son!" a Black woman with long, carefully styled hair hiccuped into a small square mic held by a tall, thin young Black man that Shekinah swore she'd met somewhere before. Maybe one of Moss's friends? The young man held a bullhorn in his other hand, connected to the square mic box by a long black coil. "The Portland Police shot Jeremy Landis down in cold blood!"

Shekinah didn't know how to feel. She stood, one arm tucked into Tish's, staring at the scene unfolding through her sunglasses, wishing she'd worn boots with flatter heels. The tarmac was hard after standing still on it for half an hour. She really should be working, with three projects in various stages of completion sitting on her light box at home.

But when she'd gotten done with yoga class that morning, Tish was waiting for her with the news that Portland police had shot a young man late the night before. There was a gathering downtown, on the spot of his murder, and Tish really wanted to go.

But she hadn't wanted to go alone. So of course Shekinah had said they'd go together, and had driven them across the Willamette to a parking garage two blocks from where they currently stood.

Standing now in front of this weeping parent and the angry, grieving group, she felt in her soul that she'd been naive. Naive, and complacent, and maybe a little bit smug in her privilege. Middle-class white women didn't usually have to concern themselves with friends and family being gunned down in the streets. Oh, there was always the threat of harassment and rape, that was real, but this?

Shekinah felt a little ashamed.

Then she noticed Tish's arm shook beneath hers.

"You okay?" she asked Tish. "Need to go?"

"No. I'm not okay, but I don't want to go, either."

"What can I do to help?"

Tish looked up at her, dark eyes rimmed with red. "Nothing."

And that was the real issue, wasn't it? There was nothing Shekinah could do but stand here. Nothing anyone could do. Oh, Alejandro talked sometimes about lobbying the mayor or city council to clean up the police bureau, and she was sympathetic, but again, she never really thought it was her issue.

"I'm sorry," she said to Tish.

"Sorry for what?" Her friend stared at the mother, who had handed the mic back to the tall young man and stood now, tears rolling down her cheeks, dabbing at her eyes with a tissue that did not look substantial enough for the job.

"Sorry for...everything." The inadequate words only served to highlight her own inadequate actions. "This must be so hard for you. After the visions."

"This is hell," Tish replied. "It's absolute hell. And it feels this way every single time. That's why the visions are so terrifying. And it's why I'm going to need you, Shekinah. I'm going to need you by my side."

Shekinah felt the words for what they were: an injunction. A charge. A demand that she do better by her friend.

Because if she couldn't, what was all the breathing, prayer, and meditation for?

"I'll be here, Tish."

Tish nodded, but didn't reply. Shekinah's thoughts swirled inside her head, disjointed and jumbled, as if she hadn't practiced earlier that morning at all. As if she had no connection to anything other than human confusion and fear.

A line from the Rig Veda flowed through her head. She whispered the words, barely audible above the shouting voices and honking of car horns.

"Formed with twelve spokes, by length of time, unweakened, rolls round the heaven this wheel..."

The wheel of time was inevitable. It rolled on, changing seasons, giving and taking lives. And her life? What was she living it for? What was her contribution to the wheel of time?

She had thought she knew. But standing on this street, in this small corner of downtown Portland, with cars honking at the disturbance to their once open pathway, she wondered if she knew anything. If she'd been wrong this whole time, to not look further past her own window and into the lives of other people.

Oh sure, she worked with the Yoga Center on the quarterly langar, or community meal, in which they fed homeless people, but who was feeding these people, here? Who was feeding them anything but sorrow and body-wracking grief and a terror she could barely begin to imagine?

She breathed in the exhaust-perfumed morning air and straightened her spine. No matter what happened, and no matter what lessons she still had to learn or whether she would teach, or lead, or not, she was a yogi, a practitioner.

And she could practice anywhere. Standing on the edge of the crowd, Shekinah began to breathe, cycling the air through her body, in, and out again.

It wasn't enough, but in that moment, all she could offer was to just be. As she breathed, she felt Tish relaxing next to her, then heard her friend exhale, matching Shekinah's pattern.

Good. That was good. Affect yourself. Affect one other person. That was a place to begin.

The cars, the honking, the shouted jeers, the sound of approaching motorcycles...none of it mattered. What mattered was breath. Presence. Being.

"Cops!" A voice cracked through the air, and Tish stiffened up again at her side.

"Damn it," Tish said. "They just can't leave us alone."

Shekinah whipped her head around, and sure enough, a row of Portland police on motorcycles had arrived.

23

ALEJANDRO

"Hey, Tempest! Good to see you." He greeted his coven mate who stood behind the counter, lock of platinum blond hair brushing her forehead, stringing satin cords through some of the less expensive medallions the shop sold. He wasn't ready to head home just yet, and had decided to look through some books, see if there was any information on symbols or sigils that would help him tune into whatever it was the ancestors were trying to convey.

"Hey there, Alejandro." She looked up from her work and gave him a slight smile. Purple shadows ringed her eyes, and they weren't smudges from last night's makeup, though he'd seen that on her in the past. These were from stress, or lack of sleep. Her skin was always pale, but she didn't usually look this...haunted.

"You doing all right?" he asked.

She shrugged one of her sharp shoulders. "I'm fine."

"I'm always around to talk, if you need it."

"I'm fine," she insisted again, then bent her head back to her work.

Now it was Alejandro's turn to shrug. You can't help people who don't want to be helped. That was something Raquel had told him before, and usually he had no trouble abiding by that maxim. But all the changes he was going through seemed to make him softer hearted. More vulnerable to other people's pain. He didn't know if that was a good or a bad thing, but it sure as hell wasn't comfortable.

Brenda had slipped into the back room behind the purple, Celtic knot work patterned curtain, and only a few other customers browsed the aisles, picking up crystals or flipping through Tarot decks. The book aisles were empty, which was good. He wasn't in the mood for smiles and politeness with strangers right now. He didn't have the bandwidth for it.

He headed to the grouping of bookshelves and the two comfy reading chairs in the center, with a small table set between them. Reaching the chairs, Alejandro looked around. Everyone was still engrossed in their own projects. Good. He closed his eyes, slowed his breathing down, and imagined the energy centers in the soles of his feet and the palms of his hands opened on his next exhalation. His body responded with slight tingling warmth where he imagined the energy centers to be.

He sent a quick thought to his ancestors, *Help me find what I am looking for*, then held his left hand out, waiting for a pull in the correct direction. He felt a tugging at his solar plexus first. Toward the right. Okay. Left hand extended, he felt the skin on his palms grow warmer as he skimmed the shelves. There. A book with a bright red spine tucked between two others. He had just slipped it from the shelf when a second, sharper, tug whipped him around to the opposite shelving unit. His hand homed right in on a slender, golden-yellow book. *Sigil Magic*, the cover read. He looked down at the other, heavier book and saw that he was holding *Mesoamerican Magic, Rituals, and Religion.*

Okay, then. Clearly these were the books he needed. *Thank you*, he thought. He couldn't wait to get home, make a quick lunch, and settle into his reading nook with the books. Not a bad plan for the day.

"I'll take these two," he said to Tempest. She rang him up with none of her usual chatter, which worried him, but he decided if she didn't want to spill, he had enough on his plate right now. Poking his head through the purple curtain, he said goodbye to Brenda, and was soon back on the street.

He was walking down Hawthorne, dodging dogs and sidewalk jewelry hawkers, wondering if he should eat something here before heading back home, when his phone buzzed. A text from Shekinah.

The cops are here.

What? he texted back. *Where are you?*

Downtown with Tish. A young man killed last night. PPB. They're...

Sweat broke out on his forehead. Damn it. Shekinah was always safe. He always knew she was safe. She never went out in the streets like this. She never...

Surrounded. SW 4th & Harvey Milk.

I'll be there.

But first he had to alert Brenda. She could tell the rest of the coven. Those who could come, would. He just wished he knew what was happening. Why was Shekinah out there in the first place?

Fingers fumbling, he fired out a text to his mentor, then half walked, half jogged toward his car. His phone buzzed in his hand. He spared it a glance. Brenda.

Wait. Let me gather some things. I'll come with you.

He slowed just enough to text back. *No time! I'll check back when I know more.*

A sense of panic rose inside him. He had to get to Shekinah, and he had to get there right away.

24

SHEKINAH

The police lined up behind them, and a mechanical voice began to bellow orders into the air. Something about dispersing.

"Tish! What should we do?"

The noise was intense. People shouting, chanting, the mechanical voice repeating its garbled phrase again and again... Shekinah felt out of her element.

"We have to move! Walk calmly. Whatever you do, don't run. Let's get to the sidewalk and try to... Shit."

"What?"

"They just blocked off the other intersection."

"But how do they expect us to disperse?" Shekinah was trying her best to remain calm, to remain in touch with her body and her breath, just like Yogi Basu taught. But her hands were clammy, her heart raced, and she tasted the bile of fear on the back of her tongue.

Tish rolled her eyes. "They don't. Let's see if there's a break in the hedge here. Get to the parking lot."

Tish pressed her hands against her temples and her face turned a grayish cast.

"Tish? What's happening? Are you sick?"

Tish shook her head. "I'll be fine. Just...let's get out of here."

They wound their way through angry, panicking people, trying to get to the sidewalk. A teenager tripped, then caught herself, stumbling into her friends who pulled her away, Shekinah hoped toward someplace safe.

Shekinah saw a break in the hedge. It looked narrow but...

"There," she said, pointing.

With a shrug of her shoulders, Tish grabbed her hand and dragged her onto the sidewalk. Her friend's hand was clammy, cold with greasy sweat. "Might be our best shot. Don't let go."

"Are you sure? You don't seem well."

"I'm not going to get any better in police custody!" Tish snapped, then turned her shoulders and started pushing her body through the sturdy hedge. Then Shekinah was in, surrounded by the sharp pressure of the manicured bushes, shoving against the green, trying to avoid getting scratched. The noise from the crowd increased, people were screaming now, and shouting at the cops. The mechanical voice droned on. It was all so loud. She fought down the rising panic. *Just keep breathing. Just keep pushing through.*

She was halfway through the hedge when Tish went limp and slumped, the stiff bushes half propping her up as she tripped toward the parking lot.

"Tish! Are you okay? Tish!" Damn it. Shekinah was trapped now. Enclosed. Nowhere to go, forward or back. Bushes scraping at her cheeks and hands, she frantically scrabbled forward, trying to get her arms around Tish's waist. Maybe she could hoist her up, get her all the way through. Get them both out of this enclosure.

Tish groaned as Shekinah grabbed her, shoving her arms between the spiny bushes and Tish's red coat. One arm around the waist, the other snaking beneath Tish's armpit, across her chest above her breasts. Bending her knees, Shekinah tried to get leverage in the narrow space. She needed to lever Tish up and see if she could walk them both out. Bracing Tish against her own chest, she barked into her friend's ear.

"Tish! If you can, I need you to help me. We need to walk forward. Get you out of here."

Tish groaned again, but when Shekinah pushed one half step forward, Tish stepped, too. Good. Another half step. Then another. Shekinah was sweating underneath her coat. Good thing Tish was light, or she'd never...and then Tish stumbled again, and fell forward, half dragging Shekinah with her. Shekinah tumbled forward out of the sharp green embrace. Onto asphalt. Grabbing Tish's head before it hit a gray concrete bumper. Her phone buzzed in her coat pocket. She ignored it.

Back aching, she eased Tish down onto the ground, cradling her head with her arms until, with a yank, she got Tish's bag beneath her head. Not the best pillow, but it would have to do. Panting, she carefully eased her spine into a standing position and stretched. Tish still looked slightly grayish, which wasn't good, and her eyelids fluttered as if someone were projecting a movie inside her head.

A buzzing from her pocket again. Shekinah pulled her phone out. It was Alejandro.

Just arrived downtown. Parked two blocks from Harvey Milk. Where are you? You okay?

She sighed with relief. No way could she move Tish by herself, not when she was collapsed like this. Dialing, she glanced around the parking lot, which was full. Tish was well hidden between cars and the hedge. The noises behind the hedge continued. Shekinah hoped everyone was okay.

And then Alejandro's voice was in her ear. She hadn't realized how much she needed to hear it. "I'm at the small street parking lot next to where all the cops are. Behind the hedge. Tish collapsed. We have to get her out of here."

And then the sound of running feet, and there he was, weaving through the cars, brow furrowed, barely looking where he was going, eyes trained on her face. He was beautiful, glasses glinting in the autumn sun. Shekinah sagged with relief and slid her phone back into her pocket.

He gave her a quick hug. "You okay?"

She just nodded, and pointed down at Tish, whose hands now covered her face. She groaned again, then rolled toward the hedge and puked.

"Shit!" Shekinah bent and tried to support Tish until finally, the heaving was done. Looking up at Alejandro she said, "Can you carry her out of here?"

"Of course." He bent and started to gather Tish into his arms.

"How far is your car? Mine is in a garage a few blocks away."

"I'm two blocks back, found a spot on the street."

"Let's go there. We have to get her someplace safe. Head to my house?"

He nodded, hoisted Tish up, and staggered into a stand, then headed back the way he came. Shekinah followed, heart still pounding, trying to calm herself.

You're okay now. Alejandro is here. You're safe.

The thought startled her. She hadn't realized how much their recent distance had affected her. Despite Maureen, her housemate, Patrick, and friends like Tish, Shekinah had felt alone. Bereft. Alejandro was the one her subconscious wanted. The one she was always reaching for. The one who lately? Just hadn't been there.

They reached his BMW.

"My keys are in my jacket. Right hand side."

She fished the key fob out and clicked the car open with a beep before racing to open the passenger door in the back. She helped Alejandro ease Tish in, then get her buckled. Tish was gone again, eyelids fluttering once more.

"I'll sit back here," Shekinah said. "Let's go to my place. Or is yours closer?"

"Mine has an elevator, and it'll be just as quick to get there from here. Would you call Brenda from the car? Let her know where we're headed? She'll want to know."

"Let's go," she said. "And thank you for coming."

He caught her mouth in a kiss, and caressed the back of her neck with his hand. "Of course I would come for you. Always."

She took in a shuddering breath and crawled into the back of his car.

Once upon a time, Shekinah would have believed he'd always come. And he had shown up for her today, hadn't he? But deep inside, the hurting part of her still didn't believe him, and wondered if he was lying to himself.

25

ALEJANDRO

Once Alejandro and Shekinah got Tish to Alejandro's place, Tish had slept for hours, finally waking around four in the afternoon. He'd made them all a quick stir fry for a late lunch/early dinner. Brenda and Raquel had just texted to say they were on their way, which was a relief. He definitely needed backup for this discussion.

He was also avoiding a text from Thomas. A sweet message that read, *Had a great time, Daddy. Would love to see you again soon.*

Tish rested, eyes closed and color better, on his leather sling chair in the library corner, feet up on the ottoman, covered by a sage-green throw. Shekinah was cleaning up the kitchen, as per their usual agreement. Whoever cooked didn't have to clean.

He sat on the couch, nursing a bitters and soda, wishing it was whisky instead. But until this evening was through, alcohol was not advised. There was too much work to do yet, and who knew what Raquel and Brenda had in store.

He glanced at the message again, before dropping his phone on the couch and taking another drink. When had he become a daddy? *The minute you decided to grow your hair out and sport a beard like some young hipster and discovered they were both shot through with silver. The minute you turned forty-five and brought a late twenty-something home.* He smiled to himself, then frowned. He shouldn't be thinking about Thomas. Not when Shekinah was clearly still upset.

They had skirted around the conversation as Tish slept, touching on it only briefly, discussing the police, the action, and visions, his and Tish's both. As Shekinah checked email on her phone, he'd thumbed through the books from the Inner Eye, searching for something that made sense, but he just couldn't concentrate. Finally, they'd settled into their old, companionable silence, sitting on the long leather sofa, his arm around her shoulders, her head resting on his shoulder as they gazed out the windows onto the city.

Now Tish was back to dozing in his sling back reading chair, and Shekinah was finishing clean up in the kitchen, because he'd cooked.

Alone on the couch, he was back with his current, free-floating anxiety as a companion. He fiddled with his phone, moving it from hand to hand.

"You can call him, you know. Or text him back." Shekinah stood behind the kitchen counter, wiping her hands on a dish towel and watching him with steady eyes. "It's okay."

"I didn't want...you were so upset." He felt tongue-tied. Stupid. When had their conversations become uneasy things? He knew the answer to that, but the reality of it startled him all the same. He'd made his partner careful around him and had become careful around her as well.

Shekinah hung the towel up to dry and padded toward the couch in her stockinged feet, jeans swishing as she walked. Her hair was down and swung gently across her shoulders, blond strands brushing at the soft gray sweater she wore, sleeves pushed up on her slender, muscular forearms. Goddess, he still loved her. Even with the distance between them, she made his heart skip a beat inside his chest.

She curled up on the leather couch, facing him. "I was upset. I'm still upset. But I think you understand why, now." She kept her voice low, not wanting to disturb Tish. "And you not talking to Thomas—not having sex with him, even —isn't going to change the underlying fact that you really need to work on *us*. Besides, making love last night helped."

Shekinah smiled and reached toward his hand that rested on the sofa back and touched his fingertips with her own. Warm. Friendly. The way Shekinah his lover felt to him. The way they felt together. Before.

A knock came at the door and Alejandro groaned, even though this was the knock they'd been waiting for.

"No rest for witches or yogis in this town," he said, then brushed his lips across her knuckles and stood to get the door.

Raquel and Brenda stood on the other side, looking like the priestesses they were. Raquel wore dark jeans that hugged her curvy hips and beneath a leather jacket, a red T-shirt sporting her café's logo. Brenda was in the same boots and leggings under long tunic and gray coat she'd worn on their earlier walk, a big purse slung over one shoulder.

"I hope you haven't been drinking," Raquel said, giving him the eye. "We have a lot of work to do."

"I know better than that." He huffed out in irritation. This wasn't starting on the best foot.

"I know you do," Raquel said over her shoulder as she walked through the vestibule, "but I also know how things have been lately."

"Hello again," said Brenda. "How's Tish doing?"

"She had us worried, and she's still a little out of it, but we got her to eat, so I think that's good. Come take a look."

They entered the common space, only to find Raquel standing in front of the weavings, practically vibrating, Shekinah at her side. Tish was still out of it in his chair.

Brenda set her purse on his coffee table and pulled out an herbal smudge stick. He caught a hint of lavender and rosemary.

"I figure Tish might need it," she said. "You, too."

"That would be great, actually."

"Stand wherever." He stood facing Raquel and Shekinah, standing stock still in front of the weavings. As the herbal smoke wreathed around his body, he felt himself relax.

"What do you see?" he asked the two women. Brenda moved around him, periodically blowing on the end of the wrapped bundle. He squinted against a waft of smoke.

"The red bars look like protection to me today." Shekinah spoke first, surprising him.

"And those arrow shapes?" Raquel chimed in. "I think Brenda was right. They feel like...like we need to prepare for battle. Like, making me wish I'd been training with the Sons of Sàngó alongside Zion, prepared."

His heart sank, but the base of his skull buzzed again. The ancestors, awake and talking, just not in words he could understand. But it seemed as if they agreed.

"What's happening?" A soft croak came from the corner. Tish was awake.

"Hey, Tish," Brenda said. "We came to check on you. How are you feeling?"

"Like a truck slammed into my head." Her voice was weak. Scratchy.

"I'll make you some tea," Alejandro said. He needed a little time.

As he put the kettle on, the three women helped Tish up from the chair, then walked her carefully to the couch, where they propped her feet up and covered her with the throw again.

Shekinah came to help him in the kitchen. She lightly skimmed her fingers over his waist, then plopped teabags into the mugs he'd set out. Orange and cinnamon spice. When the kettle was ready, he poured, and she ferried two of the mugs out to the living room. He followed with the other two. Shekinah settled on the couch with Tish, Raquel was in one of the chairs on the other side of the coffee table, and Brenda sat on a leather ottoman in front of her array of tools. He took the other chair.

"Can you tell us what happened?" Raquel asked, her voice a lot gentler than the one she'd used with him.

Tish blew across her tea, cleared her throat, and winced. "When the cops came, the visions started coming through again. I tried to hold them off, but then..."

"But then trying to get out of there, halfway through a hedge, you doubled over, and then fell."

"Yeah. The visions kind of took me over. I'm kind of freaked out by it now, but it all happened so fast..." She looked up, dark eyes huge and haunted. "And they went on for a long time. It was too much. Just too much."

Tish's eyes filled with tears, and she took a sip of tea.

"Too much how?" Brenda asked then. "Can you tell us?"

"Too many people...if we don't stop them now, they're never going to stop killing us. And the rituals? You were right. They *are* rituals. They scared the shit out of me. But the worst part? Was their faces."

Every hair stood up on Alejandro's arms. "What about their faces?"

Tish turned her head and looked straight at him.

"They were smiling. These horrible, horrible smiles."

Alejandro knew those smiles. Above the reflection of a shining tin star in his mind was a meaty, toothy smile.

He never knew it was actually possible, thought it was just some fancy phrase novelists used, but he swore the blood ran cold inside his veins.

26

SHEKINAH

After Brenda and Raquel had left, promising to see Tish safely home, Alejandro had wanted Shekinah to stay. It was tempting, that was for sure, but a sudden, driving sense had compelled her back to the Shiva Center. She needed to see her teacher again. She told Alejandro she'd be back if she could but would at least check in after her meeting.

If Yogi Basu even had time to see her.

She sat on a wooden bench in the foyer, boots off, coat hung up, breathing in the scent of incense and wood oil, waiting. Focusing on her third eye, Shekinah breathed in slowly, fingers of her right hand pointing up, thumb gently pressing her right nostril closed. Then she exhaled, still breathing through her left nostril. Slowly, the calming breath took effect, cooling the fires of stress. She felt her connection to life return as the day's tensions drifted away. In, two, three, four. Hold, two, three, four. Exhale, two, three, four. Hold, two, three, four.

Her body knew the familiar structure, and that was exactly what she needed right now. In the midst of the maelstrom of her relationship with Alejandro, Tish's visions, and the memory of feeling surrounded by police, then shoving through that tight corridor of green, fighting off panic, she needed the support of this thing she did every day. Whether the breath of fire, or this cooling breath, her body was the practice, was the prayer.

She heard the doors to the meeting room open, and exhaled in one final cycle before lowering her hand and opening her eyes. There. She was better. But she still needed to speak with her teacher. She could hear the low rumble of his voice, speaking to some yogis as he always did after class. For newer people especially, any chance for a word with their teacher was a boon. There was a time when she was like that, and then she went through a phase of avoiding him, like recently.

But tonight, the need inside her still beat strong, like the wings of a great bird inside her chest.

She waved at a few of her friends as they exited out into the cold night air. One nice thing about yogis, they were pretty good about not pushing if it was clear a person didn't want to speak. Silence was both respected and defended here.

Finally, finally, the last stragglers pulled on their shoes and boots and left the space. Yogi Basu padded toward her in his soft, leather-soled white dance slippers, one hand stroking his long beard, the other tucked behind his back, where she knew he would be fingering a mala. Always praying, her teacher. It was one of the things that made him who he was, and one of the reasons his presence felt so comforting.

"Shekinah! You were not in class tonight. Nor was Tish." He knew. She didn't know how, maybe he was psychic, or just intuited information from the way she sat on the bench, but he knew.

"May I speak with you?"

"Of course." He gestured her toward the still-open wooden pocket doors that led to the prayer and practice room. That was a surprise. She had expected to be ushered once again into the cozy womb of his office space. Entering the practice room calmed her further. The energy of the other yogis' prayers still permeated the space, along with the subtle trace of incense.

She pulled two fat cushions down from a stack in the corner and set them on the wooden floor. Yogi Basu sunk gracefully to his cushion, as though he was a person half his size. Shekinah sat with a thump. The calming breath had clearly not erased all of the tension of the day. And knowing what she had to talk about, and how unhinged it was likely to sound, only increased the tension again.

Placing her hands in prayer position in front of her, she gave a slight bow, then straightened and inhaled.

He just sat, back perfectly straight, belly resting comfortably on the tops of his thighs. His hands were on his lap, wooden mala clicking softly in the empty room. Waiting. As if they had all the time in the world.

When it became clear he wasn't going to say anything, Shekinah inhaled and exhaled once again, then tried to relax her hands, which were gripping her knees as if her knees were tiny life rafts in the midst of a stormy sea. Slowly, she uncurled her fingers, and then spoke.

"Tish is having terrifying visions, and so is my partner, Alejandro. And today, we almost got trapped by police while out supporting a family whose son..."

"Jeremy Landis."

Shekinah stopped, startled.

"You think I do not keep track of such things. But of course I do. How else can I keep this world in my mind, and in my prayers?"

"Right. We were just gathered. His mother...she was so fierce, and so broken. It was just...terrible. And then the police came, and Tish and I were trying to get away, through this hedge, when she collapsed."

"I think this was not the first time. Her spirit has been troubled, our Tish. I was waiting for her to speak with me. So why are you here tonight, instead of her?"

"She was out of it for most of the day. I hope she's finally sleeping. But also, this isn't just about the visions."

She looked up at her teacher, feeling small all of a sudden, but knowing that she had to ask.

"The Center...we feed homeless people once a month."

"As is our duty. We also feed any who come to our door."

"Yes, but..."

"But you think it is not enough?"

Shekinah felt a blush rise on her cheeks. "No. I don't. I used to, but now I see that feels selfish to me. Self-centered. Mostly, all we do is pray. Practice. But if seva—service—is part of yoga, doesn't that mean we need to look outside the self of our immediate group more often than that?"

"Ah, perhaps you are speaking of what Brahmachari Vrajvihari Sharan pointed to. 'Having faith or an under-standing of Vedantic spirituality means living social justice.' Do you feel we must act differently than we do now? Are you disputing our ways?" One eyebrow raised in its own challenge, but his eyes were still warm.

Shekinah listened to her breath, moving in and out. She listened to the stillness of the hundred-year-old building, settling around them. Then she closed her eyes, and tried to sense what was right.

She thought of the visions Tish and Alejandro spoke of, and saw the effects of those visions on her dear friend's faces.

"I think we are in the middle of a war, and more war is coming, still."

"The Kali Yuga."

"Yes. And I think that we must do everything within our power to counter that. Or at least ameliorate some of the pain and harm that comes with war." Her eyes snapped open. Her teacher's gaze was steady, unwavering. So kind. "We have more to give than we are currently offering, so yes, I challenge that. I agree. It's time we made a change. The Bhagavad Gita says 'That knowledge by which one undivided spiritual nature is seen in all existences, undivided in the divided, is knowledge in the mode of goodness.' But we feel divided. I want help. I need help."

"With what?"

"To understand what it means to act as if there is truly no division."

"And you think social justice action is the way? That we should direct the work of seva in that way? The way that our sister yogi does in Los Angeles?"

She gave a quick nod but held her tongue.

He nodded himself, a motion so brief she almost missed it.

"It is a strong thing, to challenge your teacher's school."

"I'm sorry, I...."

He held up his right hand, wooden mala dangling from his fingers. She caught a whiff of sandalwood and tried to remember the strength and fearlessness of Lord Shiva. Tried, and failed, to feel it in her bones.

"Do not apologize for attempting to speak what is true.

Now go home, bathe the toxins of this day from your skin. Sleep. We will speak again tomorrow."

Shekinah's breath stopped in her throat, just for a moment, before exiting in a rush. She rose and bowed.

"Thank you, teacher."

He rose and left the room, padding softly down the hall.

27

ALEJANDRO

Alejandro filled two cups with coffee and a dash of real coconut cream. It was morning, though the light flooding through the kitchen windows was tinged with gray. Clouds had gathered in the night and hung low over the city. The Portland rains were coming.

Last night, with impeccably strange timing—the sort of synchronicity he'd come to expect since becoming a witch—right after Shekinah had called to say she was wiped out and just needed to crash if that was okay with him, his phone buzzed. It was a text from Thomas. A sexy booty call inquiry that made him laugh.

He'd texted back *Come by* before he could second-guess himself. So this morning, sitting on a barstool at his kitchen counter, Thomas shoveled eggs with salsa and steamed vegetables into his winsome face. As Alejandro walked toward him, coffee mugs in hand, he couldn't deny how good being with the younger man made him feel. If he had to go through a sucky midlife crisis, at least he could take advantage of some of the perks.

He sipped at his coffee, wondering if he shouldn't eat something himself. Breakfast wasn't his usual, but nothing about his life lately was his usual. What was life like when he wasn't rushing out the door to move and shake some corporation, or immerse himself in code by eight in the morning? Maybe that life included breakfast. Reading the news. Scrolling through kitten gifs.

Connecting with a new lover.

"So, how long have you been a Thelemite?"

Thomas finished chewing and swallowed. "Around seven years now. Hey, don't look so surprised. I know you think I'm a child, but I'm actually thirty years old...*Daddy.*" Thomas winked one of his devastatingly green eyes.

Alejandro groaned and grabbed Thomas by the back of his neck, pulling him in for a satisfying kiss.

"Damn puppy."

Thomas smirked and went back to demolishing his eggs.

"I'm surprised I've never run into you before. The coven has done some work with Light Eternal Lodge here in town. I have a lot of respect for Frater Louis."

"I just moved up from Oakland in June and only started attending mass at Light Eternal Lodge in the past couple of months. I like the crew there, though."

Alejandro poured them both more coffee, adding thick, creamy coconut milk to both cups. None of that watery mixed crap for him.

He took a sip, thoughtful, fully aware of the fact that his ancestors were buzzing around the base of his skull and he hadn't attended to the ofrenda yet this morning. *I'll get to you soon. Promise.*

::Pay attention:: they replied.

Pay attention to what?

He felt a sharp pain in the spot where the ancestors were buzzing, as if some abuela had just smacked him with her sandal.

"Are you okay?" Thomas was frozen, loaded fork halfway to his mouth, concerned look on his face.

"Uhhh, yeah. Just thinking about too many things all at once." Alejandro grinned. "Clearly I need more caffeine."

Thomas chewed his final bite and set his fork down on the plate. "You cook a mean breakfast. Too bad you didn't eat any yourself. Thanks for feeding me."

"You're welcome. It's really my pleasure." Alejandro took another sip of coffee, then swiveled his stool so he could gaze out the huge living room windows. "You do much sigil work?"

Thomas swiveled around, half facing the windows, half facing Alejandro. "I have, but not recently." He was quiet for a moment, then held out his left arm, underside up, showing the soft skin that ran over the veins and tendons leading to his hand. "Look near my wrist."

Alejandro circled his thumb and pointer finger around Thomas's wrist, feeling the steady rhythm of his pulse. He peered at the bright colors. Yellow bell peppers. Japanese eggplant. A red stalk of chard. Was there something else? Bending closer, he saw it, inked in red. A symbol of some sort. It looked like a a stylized T.

"Tau?" he asked, recognizing the shape of the Greek letter.

"You're good. Yeah. That's my personal sigil. Most people just think it's a T for Thomas, and it is, but it's also everything represented by the letter Tau."

"The ratio of the radius and circumference of a circle," Alejandro replied.

"Right again. The dynamic between the center and the edge. But it's also the letter of life. Resurrection. As opposed to the letter theta, or death. It became the symbol of my transition. Being reborn into who I truly am. I wanted it tattooed there to remind me that rebirth is never finished."

Well shit. Alejandro sat there, gobsmacked, staring down at Thomas's arm. Rebirth is never finished. Maybe that's what all of this was about. His crisis.

The base of his skull pinged again. Insistent, as if there was something more.

Rebirth is never finished...the ancestors seemed to think this had to do with his visions. He didn't see how... There was the sharp sandal smack again.

"Ouch!" He dropped Thomas's arm and whirled toward the ofrenda. "Knock it off."

"Uh...you okay? What's going on?"

"Just my mouthy ancestors." Alejandro raked his fingers through his hair. After so many years of shaving his head to intimidate the corporate masters, it was weird having his thick hair back. "They're trying to tell me something and apparently I'm not getting the message fast enough."

"You know," Thomas replied, "I don't usually tell people about that tattoo. Makes me wonder if your people had something to do with that."

"With the way they've been acting up lately, that's likely. If you don't mind, I should probably make my offerings."

"Go for it. I'll start cleaning up the kitchen."

Alejandro gave Thomas a quick kiss, then filled a pitcher of water at the sink and walked over to the ofrenda, refilling the cups and glasses nestled on the shelves between the framed photos, flowers, and pieces of Mexican folk art. Once that chore was done, he lit some candles, pausing and breathing in the sharpness of the sulfur mixed with the spicy marigold and mellow scent of beeswax.

Blocking out the sounds of Thomas loading the dishwasher and clattering the frying pan into the sink, he concentrated on slowing his breathing down. As he exhaled, he tried to soften his ætheric body, especially in the place his skull met his neck. The place his ancestors kept crowding around. He needed to relax everything. Last night's sex had helped, but frankly, his body felt a bit battered from the visions and everything else. His spirit, too.

What are you trying to tell me? Resurrection? I know some of you were Christian, but I'm still not sure...

Pain spiked through his head. Alejandro's hands flew to his temples and he bent at the waist with a groan.

"Alejandro!" He barely registered Thomas's panicked voice before falling to his knees. *Fire. There was fire everywhere.* Barely registered the pain of bone and flesh smacking the engineered bamboo floor. Hands on his shoulders, easing him the rest of the way down. A sofa pillow, shoved under his cheek.

He was being dragged again, across the sere, dry packed earth of the Eastern Oregon desert. Hands bound. Feet bound. Shoulders wrenched. Bones rattling. Teeth biting through his tongue. Blood-filled mouth. Pain. So much pain.

That silver star, glinting in the firelight. The horrible smile.

The sharp retort of a gun. Smell of dust and cordite.

Blackness. Endless blackness. Pinpricks of starlight. The scent of green. Then black again. Warm. Safe. Close.

Then a rush of moisture. Light again. So bright. Too bright. Sharp smell of rubbing alcohol. Then a wash of color and confusion. Then...

Alejandro came to, weeping, half cradled in Thomas's arms.

"I need my phone," he croaked.

He had to call Shekinah. Tell her what he saw.

He knew what resurrection meant now. He knew exactly what it meant.

28

SHEKINAH

"This shit has to stop. Now." Raquel paced in the back room of the Inner Eye. The brightly colored banners that graced each wall of the room fluttered with each pass. Shekinah supposed they represented the four classical elements that many witches worked with. Brenda sat beneath one that was different shades of green, black, and brown, forming a mountain shape. They were pretty. Well done, actually.

It was easier to focus on the artwork than on the wild energy currently roiling off of Raquel's skin, or on the fact that her own partner, Alejandro, was curled up on a doubled-over quilt on the floor at her feet, covered by a soft woven throw blanket. She could tell he was in pain, and there was also not a damn thing she could do about it. So her eyes were wandering and her thoughts racing.

When she'd arrived at Alejandro's loft, Thomas had been half out of his mind with panic. Alejandro was rolling on the living room floor, clutching his head. He'd looked at her, lucid for a few seconds, and croaked out "Take me. Brenda and Raquel."

So, against her better judgment, she and Thomas had managed to half walk, half drag him to her car and here, to the Inner Eye. Thomas had to head off to work, or she knew he would have still been here, hovering over Alejandro's prone form.

Soft murmurs of conversation came from beyond the purple curtain leading to the store itself. Tempest had done some sort of energy work to make Alejandro more comfortable, but then had gone back to mind the shop so Brenda and Raquel could confer.

Shekinah felt agitated. Off her game. What kind of a yogi was she, if she couldn't keep her shit together? Certainly not one ready for teacher training, and nowhere near on the pathway to whatever initiation would entail.

At least, that's what you're telling yourself. Coward. Shekinah grimaced. Her inner voice was too spot on sometimes, and wasn't that annoying?

"If Alejandro's ancestors think..." Brenda began.

Raquel waved her hands, stopping her friend. Shekinah wondered if they were always like this. Able to be at odds with one another without it seeming like a threat. The way she and Alejandro used to be. Or the way she thought they were.

"I don't care what they think right now," Raquel replied. "Whatever's happening is messing up our brother Alejandro here, and is also messing with Tish, and Goddess knows how many other people. We have to figure out how to protect them! How the hell did this shit get past Alejandro's wards, anyway?"

Good question. She knew Alejandro had done some sort of ritual protection of his space when he moved in, and he said he "fed" those protections once a month, at the full moon.

Shekinah settled into the arm chair she currently occupied, one of four relatively comfortable chairs set up in what looked like a break room, but must also double as a classroom or meeting space, given the chairs stacked next to a couple of long folding tables against one wall. There was a pocket kitchen in one corner, where an electric kettle was switched on, waiting to boil. She needed to get her thoughts in order. Right now, they raced from thought to thought and thing to thing. She was no good to anyone this way.

Focusing her breathing, she fell into the familiar pattern, and closed her eyes. Brenda and Raquel could work out what they needed to on their own, and there wasn't anything she could do for Alejandro this minute. Tobias, one of the coven healers, was apparently on his way. They'd have to check in with Tish, too, to make sure nothing bad was going on there, but for now?

She entered her breath. Inhaling for a slow four count, she allowed her spirit to ride on the breath, to expand, to become spacious. And the pattern continued. As she breathed, she found her hands wanting to move. To take on shapes. Form patterns. Mudrās. Letting breath and body flow as they wanted to, Shekinah kept her attention on the fourfold pattern, and on remaining in an open state. The tension in the room bounced off her, radiating outward from her aura, not touching her core anymore. Good. That was what she needed.

Eyes fluttering beneath her eyelids, she pictured a bright, luminous spaciousness, with herself and Alejandro in the center of it. Nothing could touch them here. It was a cocoon of safety and repair. A place his soul could heal.

His soul had needed healing for a long time.

Her hands continued their search for the proper patterns. Fingers pointing upward, then down. Four fingers held together, then two. Palms up. Palms down. Symbols of wisdom. Symbols of strength. Symbols of change.

They finally settled into one form, and her attention sank like a stone. Her edges expanded, as if she could hold the world like this. A center. A radius. A circumference. The being of All.

The unbroken circle of life itself. The seed that dies, and is reborn from the darkness, becoming first the flower, then the fruit.

Alejandro.

Shekinah…

A voice came floating, as if heard through layers of water. Her attention remained centered. Her fingers still, holding the symbols. Communicating to the cosmos with two strong hands.

"Shekinah!" A voice she recognized. Brenda's voice. "I need you to come back to us. At least enough to speak."

"Something is going on with Alejandro. We need you." A smoother voice, like warm honey. Raquel.

Her eyes fluttered, blinking at the light. Shapes resolving into two faces. One pale, with dark hair in soft waves piled over a narrow face. Silver jewelry. Brenda. A darker face with high cheekbones and deep eyes. Dreadlocks coiled around it. Raquel.

And a soft, moaning sound at her feet.

"Alejandro?" Her eyes opened all the way. Her hands dropped to her lap once again. The sense of peace and protection remained.

He moaned again, then shuddered, as if every muscle in his body had tensed up. Shekinah held her hands, palms down, in the air above his body. He sighed, and relaxed, limbs uncurling themselves. His breathing deepened, as if he was drifting off to sleep. She felt untroubled, as if whatever was going wrong with him, or in the world, she could face it.

All her life, she had avoided fighting. Avoided the warrior's way. She had never felt strong enough, never felt worthy. But perhaps she had been wrong all along. Maybe this was what her teacher had tried to tell her. Why he prodded her. Perhaps this was what he prodded her toward.

Perhaps this was what it meant to be a warrior. Centered. Connected with your actions and the actions of the cosmos. Still. Focused, yet encompassing all. Able to move rightly, with certainty.

"Can you speak?" Brenda asked her.

Shekinah nodded. Then cleared her throat. She had seen something in that space beyond space, and time beyond time. A piece of information. A key.

"Alejandro." She cleared her throat again, then looked from Brenda to Raquel. "I think his soul is older than we know."

29

ALEJANDRO

His whole body felt beaten this time. Far worse than after the other visions. Were the visions getting worse? Or was the pain cumulative? His still-foggy brain barely parsed the half thoughts. The main thread running through his mind was just an awareness of the pain.

Alejandro groaned. He was on some sort of soft quilt, and covered with some other soft blanket. He fought to roll up into a sitting position. The motion made his stomach lurch. He groaned again, then eased back down. He really, really didn't want to puke. His head couldn't handle it.

"We've got a trash can near by," Raquel's voice came from near his head. A soft hand whose touch he recognized was on his shoulder. Shekinah. He could smell the incense perfume of her hair.

"Tobias is en route. He just finished with a client and is bringing some herbs." That was Brenda, speaking from across the room.

"What's happening to me?" He croaked out. "I called you...Thomas." His eyes were still closed against the lights in the room, but even through the pounding in his head, he felt his friends around him.

And then felt her. His love. His partner. She eased down onto the quilt, spooning her body behind his, just barely touching, not putting any pressure on him. Just enough to feel her warmth. She felt good. She always felt good to him, even when he was acting like an ass and pushing her away.

"Alejandro, you did have Thomas call me. That was the right thing to do. I'm glad he was with you and I'm glad I'm with you now."

His throat closed up and tears flooded his eyes. "Love you. So much."

She really was everything. Not everything in the way the songs meant it. Everything in that, she was his rock. His steady home. The light that called to him in the darkness... even when the darkness was exactly the thing he needed to explore. And she managed to do all that, be all that, and still be herself.

As the tears spilled over, running in wet rivulets down his face, he felt all of that, in one clear rush. Not thoughts. A feeling. He felt *her*.

"I see you, Alejandro. And I love who you are."

His aching body shook with release. An animal sobbing tore itself from his throat. He had a vague sense of motion, but still couldn't open his eyes.

"Too bright," he whispered.

"Damn. Of course it is." Raquel's voice.

The light dimmed behind his eyes. He slowly blinked, but closed his eyes again. Too much effort. Then someone new knelt in front of him, with the slight clank of glass and the thump of a bag. A cool hand on his forehead.

"Hey, brother. You look like shit." Tobias. His voice was

gentle and warm. "Do you think you can sit up if we help you?"

"Yes," he whispered, not wanting to nod. He blinked his eyes open again, and slowly rolled up onto his arms.

"Take it slowly," Tobias said, peering at him from beneath that one brown lock of hair that always half covered his forehead. His goatee was scruffier than Alejandro's, but he looked beautiful. Alejandro began to weep again, slow, silent tears that wet his cheeks. He let them come, too overwhelmed to feel self-conscious about it all.

Tobias and Shekinah helped Alejandro sit up on the quilt, Shekinah adjusting herself so her thighs were around his hips.

"Lean back," she said. "I've got you."

He leaned into her, gently, and released the breath he'd been holding with a sigh. He noticed Raquel hovering, trash can in hand, and smiled.

He cleared his throat. Damn. Even that hurt his head.

"I think I'm okay for now. Not going to heave anytime soon. I could use some tissue though. My handkerchief is in my back pocket and I'm not sure I can move to get it."

Raquel gave a tight, worried smile back. "I'm keeping this nearby anyway. You never know. Besides, the taste of Tobias's herbs can make anyone want to hurl."

"Hey!" Tobias said.

Brenda *tsked* and set a box of tissues on the edge of the quilt.

"Stop it, you two."

The banter showed Alejandro just how worried they all were.

"Take this." Tobias held out a dropper filled with what looked like brown sludge. Alejandro opened his mouth obediently and let his coven mate squeeze the liquid onto his tongue. Yep. Sludge. Bitter sludge. He grimaced and swallowed.

"May I?"

"You don't have to ask. Just do what you need to."

Tobias gently placed his hands on Alejandro's temples. He felt a slight buzzing that felt like bees hovering over flowers on a warm summer's day. The aching in his head slowly eased. His stomach settled the rest of the way down. His muscles still felt as if he'd been three rounds in a kickboxing match, though.

"Tempest is better at this sort of healing than I am, and you should book her for a massage if she has time."

Brenda spoke. "Once we hear what Alejandro has to report back, I can cover for her in the store."

"Shekinah? I want to take your place at his back, so I can keep feeding him energy while he talks," Tobias said. "Alejandro? Can you sit up by yourself while we make the switch?"

"Fine." Though how he was going to talk about all of this when he was barely able to grunt out single syllables, he wasn't sure.

Shekinah passed him to Tobias. His muscles screamed, trying hold him upright, and spit filled his mouth from the effort.

"Trash?" Raquel hurried it under his chin and he spat. Once. Twice. Three times. Then he paused, waiting to see if his stomach was going to rebel again. No. "Better. Thank you."

By the time Raquel took the trash can away, Tobias was in place, his fingertips resting gently against Alejandro's. Shekinah settled on the quilt next to him, one hand on his thigh.

"Can you talk?" she asked him.

"It's hard. Maybe some tea?"

"The kettle just boiled. What do you suggest?" Brenda asked Tobias.

"There's a packet in my bag. Steep two teaspoons of that for five minutes. Meanwhile, can you handle a few sips of water?"

"Yes."

Everything seemed to be taking so long. Moving in slow motion. But he couldn't make it go any faster. Water was brought. He took an experimental sip, then three more swallows.

Finally, Alejandro took in a breath. Whatever Tobias was doing was starting to help.

"I was being dragged again. And I saw that star. And the sneering, smiling face that Tish described."

"Past or future?" Raquel asked.

"Still the past. I was still back with my ancestor...and something very bad was going on. Worse even than being dragged. Worse than the fact that they were going to kill me. It was the reason they were going to kill me..."

Tears ran down his face again. He grabbed a tissue and pressed it to his mouth. How could he even speak these words out loud?

"I was part of a...ritual. Oh Goddess." Panic rose inside his chest and he began to pant.

"Sshhh," Tobias whispered near his ear. "Breathe slowly. Deep into your belly. We've got you. You're not there anymore. You're going to be fine."

Alejandro fought to breathe normally. Fought to stop the quiver in his diaphragm. Fought to relax enough that his muscles didn't seize up again.

"It was horrific," he finally got out, throat tight, his

whisper harsh with the effort of it all. "They were dancing. Leering. Circling around my tied-up body."

"You, or your ancestor?" Brenda crouched near him, face intent.

"Me. That's the thing..."

"He is his ancestor." Shekinah's soft voice surprised him. "That's what I meant, before he started shaking and moaning again and freaked us all out. He's older than we know, because he is Alejandro Guillermo. And he is Alejandro Juan."

"Reincarnation," Raquel said, speaking into the room the word that Alejandro had been refusing to hear, every time his ancestors tried to speak it. La reencarnación. A concept he didn't believe in, but here he was...

"And I was a sacrifice."

The floodgates opened and he was suddenly crying again. Sobbing like a child. Like an animal. Like a being with no thought.

His heart had broken. *He* was broken. They had broken him. And everything was pain.

30

SHEKINAH

If this kept up, Shekinah was going to need to get extensions on her current contracts. Luckily, the two projects she was currently working on were for clients she had good relationships with, and not the new start-up she had scheduled for next month.

She was back in Raquel's living room, which was currently empty of everyone except her and Alejandro. He was still too battered and out of it to go anyplace else. She sat with him on the big red couch, waiting for everyone to arrive for what was supposed to be an all hands on deck meeting. She had wanted to take him home and put him to bed, but he'd insisted that the situation was too critical to wait.

When both Brenda and Raquel had agreed, she'd backed down, after insisting that at the very least, Tempest had the chance to work on him before the damn meeting. That had happened, at least, and Tobias had sent them off with more herbs, both in tincture and tea form. It all seemed to be helping. Alejandro was looking a little more himself, though his eyes were still slightly sunken and his usually neat hair and goatee were slightly mussed and his once-pressed blue shirt was decidedly wrinkled.

She was still a little pissed off, though given Alejandro's pain levels, was trying not to show it. This damn coven always let crisis take precedence over personal needs. At least, that's the way it had started to look to her this past year. Alejandro was always running off to coven meetings, organizing meetings, and actions, or taking down domestic abusers, or any number of things. And it had all led to this. First his personal crisis or breakdown or midlife whatever. And now these visions that scared her half out of her mind.

"You aren't being fair, you know." Alejandro's voice was quiet, but she heard him anyway.

"What are you talking about?"

"I can see your thoughts, whirring in your head. And I saw the looks you gave Brenda and Raquel back at the shop. This is all my choice. Not theirs."

"But they influence you," she hissed, trying to keep her voice down. Raquel was in the kitchen, getting Zion set up with his homework. They'd called in orders for gluten free pizza and salads that should be arriving soon.

"We all influence each other. Just like you influence me and I influence you. It's part of how we live, Shekinah." He reached out and grabbed her fingertips, rocking her hand gently. Reminding her they were connected. "It's part of why we're poly, right? The world is interdependent. We're just living that out loud."

She huffed. "You're not going to get out of this with Poly 201 theory. I'm still mad at you. And at them."

He smiled. A weak smile, but a smile all the same. It was so good to see. "You mad because you're worried about me doing something I believe in versus you mad because I'm fucking up again? I'll take it."

She laughed. How could she not.

"Oh, and speaking of Poly 201, Thomas will be here tonight. With Frater Louis from his Thelema Lodge. Is that okay?"

Shekinah rolled her eyes. "After he helped me drag you to my car this morning? You think I'm worried about running into him here? Under normal circumstances, I'd say thanks for telling me, but we all of a sudden feel a little beyond that."

He shrugged.

"But lover? Thanks for telling me anyway."

Then a knock came. Either folks were starting to arrive, or the pizza was here. As she walked to the door, Shekinah had to admit that Alejandro was right. And there was also the growing sense that this was part of the warrior path work that seemed to be showing up for her, again and again, lately.

She didn't have to like it; she just had to keep breathing.

Tish was at the door and the pizza delivery person was coming up the walkway.

"Come in, come in!"

After that, the living room quickly filled, and any privacy with her partner was gone.

31

ALEJANDRO

Every coven member who could make it, plus some of their allies, arrived in twos and threes, greeting him, getting plates and napkins for the pizza, saying hello to Zion, who perched on the arm of one of the living room chairs.

Despite Alejandro's bone-deep exhaustion, it was good to see the coven. His body felt like hell, but at least his mind was finally clearing. Whatever herbs Tobias had given him, along with the energy work from him and Tempest, had really helped. Arrow and Crescent coven was a good family to have. Which reminded him, he needed to do something nice for Catarina and the kiddos. Something more than his usual.

It felt as if he was waking up from a long, strange dream, one in which he'd been wrapped in cotton wool, protected from the world. From his feelings. From stepping fully into the responsibilities he knew were his. Like setting up a fund for his sobrinos. Like doing more than giving his sister one night off a week. Like seeing Shekinah for who she truly was: not only his best friend and lover, but his full partner in life.

He'd spent so much time making money, hustling for deals, thinking that was what it meant to be an adult. Working with Arrow and Crescent had set him on the road to changing all of that. Alejandro felt almost ready for whatever his life needed to become, but they had to get through this thing first. And figuring out he might just be his ancestor, Alejandro Juan? That was going to take work as well.

Shekinah set a plate with a slice of pizza and some salad on his lap, and handed him a napkin with a light kiss, her blond hair brushing his face. "You need to eat."

"Thank you." He smiled at her, and warmth pooled inside his belly. "I love you."

She smiled back, gave him another kiss, and went to fix her own plate.

Tish sat across the room, looking haunted, barely attending to the buzz of activity around her. Tugging at the cuffs of her orange sweater, she seemed as if she might jump out of her skin at any moment. Raquel placed a hand on her shoulder and Tish jumped, before looking up to see who it was. Raquel bent to say something to her, and Tish relaxed. Just a little.

Finally, everyone who was there was settled into dining room chairs, living room furniture, or cushions on the floor. Moss and his housemates, Tariq and Barbara Jean, sat next to Selene. Thomas sat on one of the dining room chairs next to Frater Louis, a small, neat Latino man, head of the Light Eternal Lodge. Alejandro had a lot of respect for him.

Thomas had given Alejandro a quick kiss upon arrival. And as it turned out, that was just fine. Shekinah wasn't being weird, and amazingly, neither was Thomas.

Tears pricked at his eyes again. He felt damn lucky. A lot

of people didn't even have one close friend, let alone the network of support he sometimes took for granted.

"Let's get this started," Raquel said, perched on one of the dining room chairs. "We've called on some of you to help out in the past, and Arrow and Crescent Coven has helped you out on your projects, too. This one is tricky..."

She paused, and looked up at the corner of the room. Thinking. Everyone had stopped talking and munching on their pizza. Alejandro waited with the rest of the group, wondering what Raquel was going to say. He was in the thick of it, and had no clue where she was heading.

Raquel tugged on one of the thick coils of her dreadlocks. "Brenda and I have been talking, and we seem to be dealing with a nexus of powerful magic that is drawing from both the past and the future. Alejandro and Tish are having similar visions, but one is historical and one feels like premonition. As we know, premonitions only convey one possible future. We want to act before her visions come true."

"This isn't going to be our usual combination of magic and community action," Brenda chimed in. "At least, we don't think so."

"What are you thinking?" Frater Louis asked.

"While we may need community action as a screen, this battle is mostly going to be fought on the magical front," Raquel continued. "At least, that's how it looks right now. But before we get into our theories, we wanted Alejandro and Tish to share their visions. If you both feel up to it. If not..."

"I can talk," Tish said. "It's hard, but...I'm getting used to it now. The visions, I mean. The exercises you both gave me to do are really helping me deal with the visions and not freak out. So..." She exhaled.

Alejandro took a bite of his pizza. He had no desire to eat, but his body was telling him it needed the calories to make up for all of the psychic work he'd been doing, and to repair his physical and ætheric bodies. Once he crunched through the crust, he was suddenly ravenous and practically inhaled the slice. Tobias promptly plopped a second slice onto his plate. He nodded in thanks and started in on the salad.

"The visions may have started with a dream about my brother, but they've expanded," Tish was in the middle of saying. "I've seen more murders, but more disturbing than that are what Raquel and Brenda think are rituals being done by the police. It's starting to feel like we can help stop the murders by stopping the rituals."

Frater Louis set his plate on the coffee table and leaned forward, elbows on his knees, dark eyes intense. "This disturbs me. We've worked for a long time on the assumption that all divisions of law enforcement have egregores that can and should be worked against magically, but this is the first I've heard that they may be consciously formed. That police may be actually doing some form of magic. And the time aspect...will you talk more about that?"

"Alejandro?" Brenda asked.

He raised an eyebrow and held his plate out to Shekinah, who, understanding, took it from him and set it on the coffee table. He was grateful for that. Leaning and stretching still hurt, and took more effort than he currently had the energy for.

"I've also been having visions. Visceral, very real visions of one of my ancestors being tied and dragged behind horses, and of sheriffs' stars, gleaming in firelight."

"I've also had visions of law enforcement badges," Tish interjected. "Along with the weird rituals. And..." She swallowed and put down her glass of water before pressing the heels of her hands beneath her eyes.

"The shit about my brother, and the other...murders. They're tied to the rituals somehow. And they feel like they're in the future."

"Past and future," Frater Louis mused. "And here we are, making up the present as we go. So, the question is, how do we stop this future from happening, right now?"

"That's the question, isn't it?" Raquel replied.

And Alejandro knew, somehow, the answer was rooted in his past. And in the magic gathered in Raquel's living room that moment.

32

SHEKINAH

Her head reeled, and she felt on the verge of panicking.

Damn it, you're supposed to be here to support Alejandro and Tish, not melting down!

But she found she couldn't help it. And even knowing what Tish and Alejandro were going to say ahead of time wasn't helping. This group of people giving credence to the visions made them more...real, somehow. And she felt that reality thumping up against her ribs and causing bile to rise up the back of her throat. She felt like she might pass out or puke. All of her training seemed to have fled. If she couldn't even get through a meeting like this, how the hell was she supposed to become a warrior, spiritual or otherwise?

"You okay?" Alejandro's hand touched her shoulder. His voice was pitched low, to not disturb the conversation.

She shook her head. "No. I'm sorry but, I'm...I don't know what's happening to me."

"Shekinah?" Brenda's voice carried easily across the room, and Shekinah realized the others had all stopped talking and looked at her with various expressions of puzzlement or concern. "What's wrong?"

She shook her head again, then leapt up, slamming her shin into the coffee table, rattling the dishes. She ran to the bathroom down the hall and fell to her knees in front of the toilet as dry heaves convulsed her body. It felt as if a snake gripped her intestines and was trying to exit her body, but nothing came up but bile.

Spitting one last time, still kneeling in front of the white toilet in the white and blue bathroom, she began to repeat a phrase. It was another from the Rig Veda that she hadn't thought about in a long time. "Only the person having firm conviction and iron volition can attain strength and energy. At no stage of Karma does he ever hesitate."

She hadn't felt this frightened, or this weak, in years. Not since she first stepped inside the Shiva Center and almost ran back out again. She knew then that her life was about to change, in a big way. And that's what this felt like, too. Her teacher must have known it. Must have seen that an initiation was already taking place inside her.

"Give me conviction and iron volition," she prayed. Shekinah never thought she'd reach a point in her life where she was praying on a bathroom floor. But here she was.

"Shekinah?"

She pushed herself up from the tiled floor and turned. Raquel stood by the door, face filled with compassion.

"A bit much?"

Shekinah turned on the cold water tap, splashed her face, and rinsed her mouth. Raquel held out a blue hand towel. Shekinah mopped at her face and then looked into the mirror. Her eyes were rimmed with red and she looked ghostly pale, washed out from her skin to the blond hair that hung like limp snakes around her head.

"Mouthwash in the cabinet if you need some."

Shekinah took the small bottle down, tipped some in her mouth without touching her lips to the bottle, and swished the medicinal minty liquid around before spitting and rinsing again.

"Thanks. Yeah, it's all a bit much. But I'm ready to go back now." She folded the towel and set it on the side of the sink. "Thank you."

She followed Raquel back into the living room.

Alejandro held out a hand to her. She took it, and let herself be pulled in for a gentle kiss, but not before she saw the wince of pain even that small gesture caused him. Damn. She really needed to not fall apart.

"What happened?" he asked.

"You don't have to talk about it if you don't want to," Selene said quietly.

"Actually, I'm afraid she does," said Frater Louis. "I'm sorry. I know I'm a guest here, but if we're going to figure out how to approach this, we need all of the information available."

Shekinah held up a hand to forestall any more protests. "You're right. You're right. Just give me a moment."

Settling into the couch, she crossed her legs beneath her, straightened her spine, closed her eyes, and placed a finger against her left nostril. She did three slow cycles, in and out before letting her hand drop and opening her eyes. Better.

She looked around the room. Everyone just waited for her to start. Some munched on pizza or drank fizzy water. Others just sat, quietly. These people really were trained, just like yogis. Shekinah felt kind of stupid for assuming that because their practice was different, they were undisciplined. Even though she knew what Alejandro's practice was like, she had figured that was just him. Feeling herself blush, she cleared her throat, took a drink of her own fizzy water, and began.

"At first, it felt like I was going to have a panic attack. But then..." She looked up at the bright painting above the mantel. "It felt as if a giant snake started squeezing its way out of me."

"You are a kundalini practitioner?" Frater Louis asked.

"Yes. But this felt different than the energy I usually work with." Or had it? "Well. Wait. That's not exactly right. It was just as powerful, but harsher. I really don't know what it was, or what it means. I need to talk with my teacher about it."

"Okay," Raquel said. "We have cops, sheriffs, rituals, murder premonitions and flashbacks, and snakes. Where in the ancestor's names does that leave us?"

"Needing to track down the Portland Police egregore," Moss said. "That has to be it, right? And then we need to figure out how they're feeding it, and why."

"We know why," Raquel snorted.

"Well. Yeah," Alejandro butted in. "We know why. Control. But why *this* escalation? Why this crossroads? Why now?"

"The new police chief," Moss half whispered.

The small hairs on the back of Shekinah's neck rose to attention.

"The two snakes," she said. "There are two snakes, sometimes three. Twining together. Maybe he brought a snake of his own."

"And it joined with the one that was already here," Raquel said. "And together..."

"Synergy," Shekinah replied. "More power than they ever had before."

33

ALEJANDRO

"The ancestors showed us two patterns, one for offense, one for defense," Alejandro said.

Most people had cleared out of Raquel's home, leaving Frater Louis, Thomas, Alejandro, and Moss in the living room. Raquel, Brenda, and Shekinah were up in the attic ritual space with Tish, trying to get more insight into what the rituals both he and Tish had been getting flashes of might be. The more they knew, the better able they'd be to target their magic.

Alejandro was starting to get the sense that most of this battle was going to be fought on the astral plane somehow, but that didn't mean they didn't also need to work on protecting the community, as best as they could.

"Can you show us?" Frater Louis asked.

Alejandro found the photos on his tablet and passed them over.

"The energy behind these is good, but the symbols themselves don't feel quite right for our purposes. What do you think? Should we design some sigils based around these?"

"I think we'll have to," Moss interjected. "For one thing, we don't know if the symbols in the weavings were for that community at that time, or were more generalized. But they feel pretty specific to me."

Alejandro found himself nodding. "I think Moss is right. And yeah, two sigils feels right to me. Something easy to use."

"Something we can post around town," Moss said.

"We need to let the cops know we're on to them," Frater Louis replied. "Maybe the symbol of an all-seeing eye?"

Thomas had been sketching as they talked. "How about something like this?" He held out his notepad. There were several symbols doodled on the page, but at the bottom right, he'd circled the one he was pointing toward.

It was a simple triangle with an eye in the center. Beneath, in block letters, he'd written ALL EYES ON YOU. Alejandro shivered just looking at it.

"Damn. That's good. It's not even charged up yet and I can feel it."

Frater Louis scratched at his chin. "I think we can work with that. But how about the protection symbol? I don't want to choose something from a specific culture, because the attacks aren't on any one sector. But like this one, it needs to be simple. Easy to read and to draw."

"I'm happy to sit here and work on it if you all want to keep talking strategy," Thomas replied.

They left him to it.

"Once we get the symbols right, we'll need to charge them up. Make copies. I can get a crew to help tape them up around town. We'll need to be careful in the areas the cops congregate and be on the lookout in general. I'd like groups of three or four," Moss said.

Alejandro was really tired. After this meeting he needed

to get back to his condo to crawl into bed. He started wishing he had a cup of coffee. He rubbed the bridge of his nose and tried to refocus.

"How do you want to charge them?" Frater Louis asked. "We could do something at our lodge, if you want."

"We've got a big holiday coming right up," Alejandro said.

"You all don't have something else planned?" Frater Louis asked.

"We did," Alejandro said, taking a sip of fizzy water. "But since the ancestors are a big part of this, Samhain seems like the right time for the working. They're the ones who seem to be driving this bus, anyway."

"And we should probably go out right after ritual and start hanging the fliers around town," Moss said.

That was a good idea. Alejandro felt the pressure growing around him again, felt the ancestors clamoring around his skull, and became aware of the certainty of his ancestor—that was now a part of him?—growing within his solar plexus.

This is what I'm meant to do. Who I'm meant to be? That was the feeling settling in around him. But part of his brain rebelled. The piece of his personality that was attached to things being rational, and to having a clear path forward.

What the hell are you talking about? that part of him argued back. *How is this going to help me or anyone else? And how is it going to keep food on my table, or take care of my sister's kids?*

::You need to learn to listen better. You have grown too brittle. Be supple, like the willow tree. Be strong, like the oak. Do not let fear and uncertainty break you.::

Was that what he'd allowed to happen? Was that why his whole life had needed to fall apart?

::Some structures must be torn down and be rebuilt again in order to serve their better purpose.::

The ancestors' words permeated his being, flowing like warm honey through his veins. He felt the truth of them, and not only for his current life situation.

"This magic we're about to do, it's the beginning of a much larger piece of magic," he said. "The ancestors are showing me things...dealing with this egregore, and the layers of ritual magic that are part of this? It's the first step to restructuring so many things."

"Like what?" Moss asked.

"It's the first step toward abolition, and the beginning of a cycle that will bring us something new. Something so different I can barely start to imagine it. I'm sure some of your radical friends have ideas, though."

Moss blinked, eyes bright with unshed tears. Alejandro felt moved, too. He sagged with relief to know that this crisis he was in wasn't actually centered around him. Oh, that was part of it, certainly. As above, so below, and all that. As within, so without. But the fact that it also rippled out into a much larger change? That was so much better. He wasn't just navel gazing and fucking up his personal relationships. He was also helping to do one small part to shift the balance in the world.

"How about this?" Thomas held up his notebook again. Drawn large on a fresh page was a square with a circle inside. The whole image was divided into four quarters by an equal-armed cross. Beneath the bottom line of the square were written the words STRONGER TOGETHER.

Looking at it, the whole thing filled Alejandro with a sense of rightness. Correctness. Of something true.

"How'd you get there?" Frater Louis inquired.

Thomas flipped back and held up two pages of what

would look like chicken scratch to anyone not used to constructing magical sigils.

"I just started writing the letters over each other, one on top of the other, until the basic shape emerged. I didn't even bother with the cross-out letter method, though I could have used that, here. I just kept tracing the letters over and over, as the words are written."

So, they were literally looking at a sigil made of the words "stronger together." It was classic chaos magic that had resulted in a structured, ceremonial-looking sigil.

"It's brilliant," Alejandro said. "It feels just right."

The ancestors hummed quietly at the base of his skull. It seemed that they agreed.

34

SHEKINAH

The white, triangle vault of Raquel's attic ceiling abutted knee walls covered in bookcases that held what looked like ritual supplies, extra cushions and, well, books. Shekinah sat on a bright cushion next to Tish. Brenda and Raquel sat across from them, forming a rough square.

The room felt good, which went a long way toward soothing Shekinah's anxiety. It looked as though Tish was feeling similar effects. Her face was less pinched, and her skin was closer to its usual rich tone, reflecting the warmth of the orange sweater she wore over indigo jeans. The ghostly scents of unfamiliar incense and beeswax were comforting. Not exactly homey, but reminiscent enough of the smells she was used to that they made Shekinah feel at home.

"So," Brenda was saying, "the primary connectors to the visions seem to be the five- and six-pointed stars, and the impression of fire."

"And the sense of urgency. And fear," Raquel said. Shekinah had the impression that if there had been enough ceiling height up here to pace, Raquel would have been doing so now. They had chosen to meet up here because Alejandro was still too battered to make the climb.

"We have all of that to work with, then." Brenda made some notes in a green leather-bound book. Must be some sort of magical workbook or record. When Shekinah had begun her kundalini practice, she'd kept a spiritual journal, but had fallen away from the practice in the past few years. Maybe she should start it up again. It might help her navigate the current weirdness.

"Work with how?" Tish asked. "I still don't see what we can do with either my visions or Alejandro's ancestor stuff. And, while I'm relieved you're all on board, I'm still scared for my brother's life."

Raquel reached a hand out and squeezed Tish's shoulder. "Of course you are. We live with that fear every day even without the sort of visions you're having, don't we? But the thing about witches is, we can take the information visions give us and learn to act on it. We can do ritual, if necessary, and we can also work with the images and feelings you're having up on the astral plane."

"I still don't understand."

Shekinah didn't, either, so she was glad Tish was here to ask the questions.

Raquel closed her eyes and, two deep breaths later, Shekinah felt the woman's energy change. She felt more tangible somehow. More present, focused, and alive. Despite their energy being different, right now, Raquel reminded her a little of Yogi Basu.

Raquel opened her eyes. The rich brown seemed to have added depth now, too, as if Raquel was peering into another world and seeing things in the attic room at the same time. Shekinah shivered slightly, and wrapped her arms around herself, feeling the softness of her gray sweater, the texture of it anchoring her to the familiar.

"It's like this," Raquel said, eyes trained on Tish, who sat, rapt, hands resting loosely on her knees. "The world as we know it is part of many other worlds, seen and unseen. The world of plants, animals, and insects that we think we know but don't really. The world of various Goddesses and Gods. Other spirits. The world of possibility. The world of illusion. Woven among these worlds is a thing we call the æthers, or the astral plane. In actuality, that has many levels, too. It's not just one, contiguous space. But we can work there. Free our consciousness from our physical bodies and travel to these other spaces sometimes."

Tish shrugged. "I'm going to have to take your word for it."

"You don't have to believe anything," Brenda assured her. "We respect healthy skepticism, and often tell our students to act 'as if.' For the ancient Greeks, imagination was a real thing, not just make believe. We rely upon imagination a lot."

Shekinah had to admit she felt relieved. She understood altered states, and was fine with talk of God and energy changes and all the rest of it. But she also didn't want to all of a sudden have to believe in a bunch of alternate realities in order to help out Tish and Alejandro. And the city of Portland, if it came to that.

But didn't she deal with alternate realities all the time? Maybe that's what altered states of consciousness were. Tapping into alternate realities.

"Alternate ways of being." The words were out of her mouth almost before she thought them.

Brenda flashed her a smile. "That's as good a way of explaining it as any. Whatever works for you is fine. We just need to know you aren't going to freak out when things get strange."

"I'm a Black woman in a seventy-five-percent white city. My whole life is strange," Tish said.

Raquel laughed, a big boom that hit the rafters. Shekinah couldn't help but grin, and chuckle a bit herself. The sound of laughter was a welcome relief.

"I'm serious, though," Tish continued. "Any weird stuff you want me to do? If it's going to keep my brother alive, I'm in."

The smiles left all of their faces.

"So, then. Here's what I think we should do," Raquel said, leaning forward. "We're going to take their symbols and mirror them with our own. They're the same stars, right? And we're going to use those as portals..."

35

ALEJANDRO

"I'm scared." His head was cradled in his favorite spot between Shekinah's shoulder blade and her collar bone. Her arm was wrapped around him, and he could just barely hear her heart, beating beneath her ribs. They lay on top of his comforter, still dressed except for their shoes. He wished he'd thought to pull on some sweats before flopping down, but had just been too damn tired, after the day, then the meeting, and the second meeting after that, trying to figure out the sigils.

His bedside lamp cast a warm glow on her skin, and some old Psychedelic Furs played softly. "The Ghost in You." Comfort music from middle school, when puberty first gripped his body. He'd slowed down since then, but not much. Sometimes he still felt like that twelve-year-old boy inside.

And come to think of it, that song title hit a little too close to home, considering it might turn out he was actually the ghost of his murdered ancestor. Or something.

"I am, too, babe. We'd be stupid not to be."

"I'm sorry I dragged you into this."

He felt the huff of air, the sharp rise and fall of her bones. "You *really* think you dragged me into this?"

Alejandro shifted slightly, pushing himself up enough to see her face looking down at his, the eleven-shaped crease between her brows deepening as she frowned.

"You really think," she continued, "that no one else is going through shit of their own? That this has nothing to do with things going on in my own life, with my teacher? Or with Tish coming into her psychic powers, or anyone else who was in that room tonight? Uh-uh. You are not taking responsibility for this. That's just rude."

He flopped down on his back beside her. Rude? How was he being...?

"You always think you're the one driving the bus, Alejandro, and frankly, I think that's why you've pulled away lately. You never want to ask for help. I'm your *partner*. I want you to treat me like one again."

Frustration warred with sorrow in his chest. He closed his eyes. Corralled his breathing. Tried to ignore the sense of being dragged across hard earth. The flickering of flames. He hadn't lit any candles tonight. Couldn't bear to. It was Alejandro Juan's memories, dancing through him still. He tried to take comfort in the feel of his lover beside him, but couldn't get it back.

A sharp need pierced his belly. He wanted Thomas. He wanted someone new, someone who didn't know him like Shekinah did. Someone who, therefore, was just more *simple*. Someone he could take care of, maybe, instead of needing...

"Shit."

"What?" He heard her shift. Even with his eyes still closed, he could tell she was looking at him.

"I'm sorry. You're right. I just realized I'm scared of more than just the fact that I might actually be the damn reincarnation of an ancestor that was ritually killed by law enforcement. And how fucked up is that?"

He opened his eyes again, and stared at the white expanse of his bedroom ceiling, hand snaking across the few inches of sheet to grab Shekinah's hand. She curled her pinky finger into his. Companionable. Friendly. Loving, even though he was being difficult.

"So, what's this revelation you just had?"

"I've been flailing and, you're right, pushing you away, and that's because whatever this initiation is that both of us now seem to be going through? It's about ripping away another layer of protection, getting closer to the core. Closer to reality. Closer to the truth."

He felt her body grow still, heard her breathing, slow and even, rising and falling along with the music.

"Well," she whispered. "Damn." She moved then, scooting up, grabbing an extra pillow, and propping herself against the gray padded headboard. He followed suit, though it hurt, he had to admit. He wanted nothing more than to soak in the tub. But this conversation needed to be had.

"I'm scared of needing you as much as I do," Alejandro said. And his heart was racing, and it was hard to even take a breath. Raising his hands to his face, he cupped his palms over his eyes and pressed, trying to keep the panic at bay.

"Lover, you don't have to..."

"But I do." Alejandro swallowed. All of a sudden, he felt as if he had no access to any of his practices. No access to centering, deep breathing, to opening the energy centers in his hands and feet... All of it had fled. There was just this sense of naked panic, Shekinah lying at his side, waiting. And then there were the ancestors. Those fuckers were pressing at the base of his skull, buzzing and clacking and making themselves known.

This isn't going to get any easier, he thought.

"I'm so scared that it's all going to overwhelm me," he said. "I'm scared it's going to smother me."

"This need?"

Finally, Alejandro lowered his hands and blinked, only to see her beautiful face gazing down at his. That helped, but only a little.

"It's that, but it's not just that. It's everything. It's the fact that I'm not only having these horrific visions, but that I might actually *be* my ancestor. That's just something I never thought of. I've always been an agnostic about the afterlife, you know? And to have this... It's too much. Add in the fact that I'm having a crisis about work, and a crisis with *us*, and with me acting out, feeling like I want to go back to when I was in my twenties or thirties—which is ridiculous! Because I *don't* want that!"

"You just want Thomas," Shekinah quipped.

He laughed at that, a dry chuckle, without too much actual laughter in it. She knew him too well.

"Yeah, I want Thomas, but the thing I just realized? Part of what I find so hot about Thomas right now is, not only does he want me, but I don't have to be vulnerable with him like I do with you. I don't have to bare my soul, or, you know, let him know who I really am. I can just be his handsome daddy and have some fun."

He looked into her amazing, liquid blue eyes. "I've been avoiding you, and I'm so sorry. I've just...I've just felt lost. And I think that pissed me off. And, I didn't want to take that out on you, but I also..."

Goddess, this was hard.

Shekinah ran a hand across his forehead and through

his hair, trailing her fingers across his scalp. It felt good. Comforting. Funny, it was nice to feel fingers in his hair after having shaved his scalp for so long. That felt vulnerable, too, though. Exposed. As if he were a little boy needing comfort. Thing was, he supposed that was true.

"I want to do better," he said. "I want to try harder. With you, with the coven, with everything. But I'm so fucking afraid. I'm afraid I'm going to lose it. I'm afraid I'm going to lose it all."

"Come here," she replied, and gathered him into her arms. She held him, gently, so, so gently. Alejandro shifted his head, tilting his face toward her.

She brought her own face down for a kiss that started out as gentle, but quickly grew in heat.

"You're not going to lose this," she said, after breaking their kiss. And then she began to unbutton his shirt, eyes never leaving his.

"Goddess, you're beautiful."

She smiled, a radiant thing. "Don't ever forget it."

As he moved to help her, stealing hot kisses in between each article of clothing, he vowed to himself that he never would.

Alejandro allowed his aching body and battered spirit to sink into motion and sensation, pleasure, and a love so strong it took his breath away.

36

SHEKINAH

Shekinah sat next to Tish on a bench in Lownsdale Park, one of the three South Park Blocks in downtown Portland. This one sat across from the main courthouse, one block from City Hall. People wandered through the park, heading out to lunch or back to the office, walking in pairs and trios or scurrying along alone. A few houseless people sat in a circle on the grass on a carpet of fallen leaves.

The air was chilly, and she was grateful for her sweater and jacket. She and Tish were waiting. For what, Shekinah wasn't certain. All she knew was that Tish had asked to meet her there. Said that it was important. At least her morning practice had been good and Shekinah had gotten some work done that morning, which would make her clients happy. Her stomach grumbled. She really should have eaten some lunch before coming here.

A small group held signs near the edge of the park closest to the courthouse, clustered around three African American women. She couldn't read their signs, but Shekinah recognized one of the women from the street protest.

"They look so sad," Tish said, her gaze trained on the

group. "They're the reason I wanted you to come here. To stand with them. Or talk to them. Or..."

She looked at Shekinah, her own eyes damp with tears, mouth set tight, Shekinah couldn't tell whether it was from grief or anger. "Frankly, I'm not sure why I brought us here. I just knew, after last night, that we had to come. They're the ones this bullshit is affecting. They're the ones this magic or whatever it is keeps jerking around."

Tish looked back at the group, Shekinah's eyes followed. One or two people paused to read their signs, and one spoke with a person on the edge of the small cluster. Most people, though? They walked on by.

"That woman there?" Tish pointed to a woman sitting on her walker chair, sign facing toward the sidewalk. "Her grandson was killed by the Portland police two years ago. She's been organizing ever since. Most of the people there? Family members killed."

Shekinah's eyes filled with tears, and she touched Tish's arm. Tish turned to her and shook her head.

"Makes me want to cry, too, but they don't need your tears, Shekinah. We don't need your tears. We need your action."

Tish turned her head away again.

Shekinah exhaled, mind awhirl. She didn't speak, because what the hell could she even say? She felt so out of her depth here.

"I'm thinking of quitting the Center," Tish said.

"Why?"

She shrugged. "I don't see how it's helping anything. These visions...they have me questioning everything, you know? Like, if yoga helped anything, I wouldn't be having these visions. Wouldn't need to."

"Doesn't practice help *you*, though?"

"I thought it did, but now I wonder…"

Looking at the bereft and angry families, standing in the small park, holding signs, Shekinah wondered what she could do. What would help.

"Conviction and iron volition," she said.

"What?" Tish replied.

"From the Rig Veda. That's what we need here, to help with the magic. To turn the stars back on the police. To help these families. We need conviction and iron volition. The power to use our will. Our holy power. All of the kundalini we've been raising all these years, but harnessed toward something."

"Sounds great," Tish replied, "but how?"

"I don't know yet," Shekinah said. "But we're going to figure it out. Meanwhile, should we join them?"

"Yeah," Tish said, standing up. "Let's go."

As they walked toward the group, Shekinah felt a sense of purpose, rekindled inside her belly.

She just hoped it would be enough to help.

37

ALEJANDRO

It was early evening, and twilight was falling, along with the temperatures. Alejandro walked into the indoor space at the Mercado, holding the door for his sister and her kids. Music hit him. The sounds of accordion and twelve string guitar filled the air.

The Mercado was busy, with the after-work crowd coming by for dinner or to visit the ofrendas. Alejandro and his family were doing the same. The kiddos had already consumed their burritos from one of the food trucks outside, eating at the long tables under strings of party lights. He and his sister had shared a plate of grilled meat, beans, rice, and salad with a side of fried yuca. Bellies comfortably full, they now wandered the indoor marketplace, visiting the large, vibrant ofrendas.

The subtle, spicy scent of marigolds mixed with the food smells rising from the few small inside tables where folks were eating.

His sister looked beautiful but tired as usual. He worried about her. They argued about her working too hard, but she was proud and wouldn't allow him to give her and the boys any steady income. Stubbornness ran in the family. So he did what he could.

He'd suggested this trip because two nights from now, on Dia de Los Muertes, he knew he would be busy. That was the evening the ancestors had decreed. It was the night Arrow and Crescent Coven and their allies would work their magic against the egregore of la policía. He'd meet with the coven later on but didn't want to miss this traditional visit to the Mercado with his sobrinos.

How was it already Samhain? He'd spent the day getting the sigils ready. He, Thomas, and Moss had met with Shekinah, who had turned the hand drawn symbols into vector files on her computer. That way they could easily scale the images up and down for large fliers or small, unobtrusive squares. Moss had complained that he wished they had time to make stickers, until Thomas reminded him that once the sigils themselves were charged up, they would work for as long as they needed them to. Stickers could come later, even after the current action they had planned.

An action Alejandro was still uncertain of, and which made him feel increasingly nervous. He hated flying by the seat of his pants. That had never been his way. Not in business. Not in relationships. Not in his magic. Even the actions the coven had done in the past all had some external event to center themselves around, to anchor to.

Right now? There was nothing in his life that had the sort of structure that made him feel as if everything was going to be all right. His only anchor right now was the longevity of his relationships with Shekinah and the coven. He hoped that would be enough, and that he'd find the inner strength to make it through.

"Tío, look!" His nephew Joey pointed to a floor to ceiling

ofrenda, brimming with marigolds, paper flags, and folk art skeletons. It was four tiered, and jar candles flickered in front of old photos. These were Oregon ancestors. Farm workers and vaqueros. Men and women who worked on the railroads. All the people who had been brought here, or traveled on their own, who had settled and then fought to remain here. The more recent photos were of activists from the 1960s on up through the 1990s. Joey was pointing to an old photo, a sepia image of a man with sad, dark brown eyes, a full mustache, and hair as thick as Alejandro's. Sudden heat ran across Alejandro's skin, stopping him in his tracks. The base of his skull buzzed with activity. The man wore the clothing of a cowboy, though it was clear he had dressed in his best for the photo.

"He looks like you! Is he part of our familia?"

Alejandro cleared his throat. "I believe so, sobrino. He certainly looks like it."

Well, shit. People talked about what to do if you met your doppelgänger, but what in Goddess's name were you supposed to do if you were looking at your past self? How was this even possible? Staring at Alejandro Juan's image— it had to be him, didn't it?—made his stomach lurch, as if time had suddenly shifted, leaving him half in and half out of his body in this place and time. His hands reached out as if to grab the photo from the shelf. He wasn't sure if he wanted to smash it or steal it away.

"Alejandro, are you okay? You don't look so hot. Did you eat too much?" Catarina asked.

"I'm not sure what's wrong," he lied, "but you're right, I don't feel so well."

She made a flicking motion with both hands. "Go. Go."

"But..."

"It's okay, Tío, if you feel sick, you shouldn't be around

people anyway. That's what Mom always says," Henry chimed in.

He gave his family what he hoped looked like a smile instead of a grimace.

"I'm sorry. I'll make it up to you next week."

Dropping kisses on the tops of their dark heads, he made his way through the long tables filled with ofrendas, heading toward the door.

It was probably just his imagination, but it felt as if that photo of Alejandro Juan stared at his back the whole way.

38

SHEKINAH

"I want to take kundalini practice to the streets," she said.

It took all she had in her to remain seated in the chair in front of Yogi Basu's desk. Her practice that morning had left her the most energized she'd been in months. She practically vibrated with the energy flowing through her body and across her skin. If she hadn't been seated, Shekinah swore her feet would levitate off the wooden floor. The portrait of Shiva looked down upon her. Shiva—who destroyed so things could be created anew—was the reason she was here now, the reason she practiced. The reason she felt this sudden urgency to *do* something. Maybe this was what being a warrior felt like.

Her teacher stroked his beard thoughtfully, his gaze steady.

"This is the moment I have been waiting for, Shekinah. I have waited for the serpents to open you to the fulfillment of your cause."

"I don't... I have no idea what you mean," she said.

"I think you do know. I think you will find that you know, if you look inside your heart. This opening is what you've been so frightened of. And it is why the excuses have filled up your heart and mind. Being so full like that has meant you cannot listen clearly. You have not been listening to me, or to your practice, or to yourself."

Words pushed at the back of Shekinah's lips, trying to break through the fortress of her teeth. But she held them in. Forced herself to feel her feet on the floor, her butt muscles in the chair, and her spine rising up from her pelvis. She could feel them now, two serpents where before there had been only one. How had she not recognized that before? That there were *two* serpents twining their way through her? Oh, she knew the teachings. She had seen the illustrations. Shiva and Shakti. And when both were fully present, the possibility of Sushumna, which was beyond all concepts of duality.

But nonetheless, in her practice, she had always felt the kundalini rising up her chakras as only one force, not two. She had been focused on Shakti, but after all these years, Shiva had awakened inside of her.

That energy, a second stream of life force, flowed through her now.

She touched the tip of her tongue to the roof of her mouth and spread her toes out on the floor.

"Do not try to control this," her teacher said. "Rather than trying to slow down the flow, imagine that your energy field can expand to accommodate it. To accommodate the powers as they rise."

How did he do that? Even after all these years, it was still spooky, the way he could read her so accurately.

Shekinah breathed in, and as she exhaled, she imagined her breath pushing itself outward, all around the edges of her skin. Then she imagined it spreading itself, layer upon layer, all around her. Above and below her. In front and behind her. Side to side.

What would it be like to feel bigger? she thought.

And so, she *did* imagine it. She imagined herself taller and broader, larger all around. Big as a mountain. An ocean. A sun. The energy rose inside her, from feet, to pelvis, and up. As soon as it reached her heart, something clicked inside of her with an almost audible snap. All the facets of her self—body, mind, and soul—aligned. And all the tension she'd been feeling was simply gone. The vibration that had threatened to overwhelm her steadied into a gentle, powerful thrum.

The center of her forehead tingled, and she felt something open wide, like a beautiful flower. Joy filled her, and a new sense of her power.

She looked into the bottomless pools of Yogi Basu's brown eyes, and in a steady voice she said, "I think I understand now."

He simply nodded, as if of course this would have happened, this thing that she was certain had just changed her entire life.

"To answer the question you asked earlier," he said, "the kundalini is already in the streets, though not in all places. The kundalini flows everywhere that creation is unblocked. Practice, as you know, is one way to release these blocks, and practice is what the universe does. We practice with everything that practices."

She could taste the truth of his words in her mouth, feel the rightness of them, though her brain could not have explained in a million years what exactly he meant.

So, she just nodded.

"But the people need our help. Now. These visions…"

"We will find a way," he said. "Thus far, it has not been

my practice to do more than teach and pray." He waved a hand in the air. "Oh, yes, we do the langar every month, but that is simple duty, to feed people in need. And I believe you are asking for something more. Let me pray upon this, let me ponder."

"Thank you, teacher. I will pray and ponder, too."

She rose and bowed slightly but couldn't make herself turn toward the door. Praying and pondering weren't enough. Not right now. There had to be something more... Something simple. Something the Center was already doing.

"Was there something else, Shekinah?"

His voice startled her, and she realized she'd been staring at the painting of Shiva, as if he had an answer for her. And perhaps he did.

Her teacher waited, completely patient and still, though she was certain he had one hundred other things he should be attending to.

"You reminded me that kundalini flows every place there is an opening... And we talked about the importance of seva, and social justice. But we never finished that conversation."

"Yes?"

She swallowed, and felt the outstretched palm of Shiva, lending her courage.

"I want to make more openings. To bring our meditation to the streets. Or can we ask the Center to direct their prayers toward an end to police violence? Or something—anything—more direct than what we've been doing? That's what I'm asking. And I really need an answer." She knew it was risky, pushing her teacher like this, but even scared and feeling slightly sick, she also knew that it was right.

She just hoped he saw that, too, and heard the desperation she knew was in her voice.

Her teacher steepled his fingers and pressed his fingertips to his lips. It was her turn to wait this time.

She stood, he sat, and Shekinah felt the moment when their breathing synchronized, his exhalation becoming her inhalation, his inhale drawing from her exhale. The energy in the room shimmered slightly around her. Her eyes flicked to Shiva's portrait. His halo seemed much brighter than before.

"Your idea has merit. If you find an action where we can go pray, or to feed more people, we shall do so. As for asking people to make directed prayers? I will think about how to best do this thing."

He sighed. She had never heard him sigh before, though, human as he was, certainly things must weigh on him just like they did on her.

"You are good for me, Shekinah. You remind me what it means to be a warrior in more than simply spirit. You remind me of my duty."

He pushed back from his desk and stood.

"And you are right, the teachings say that we must practice both spiritual and physical powers. Especially in these times."

Coming around his desk, he startled her by holding out his hand. Shekinah paused for a moment, then took a breath, slid her palm inside of his, and shook.

"Thank you for your forthrightness," he said. "I hope to be training you to teach others soon, as you have just taught me."

Blinking back tears, all she could do was bow over his hand.

Then, amazingly to herself, she simply turned and

walked out the door. Everything felt as if it was simultaneously brand new and yet, still ordinary. As if nothing was different at all.

Except for two things. There was the new certainty that she was one with the cosmos, and therefore her part of the cosmos could change. And she'd had enough courage to speak up about that, and her teacher had listened.

39

ALEJANDRO

The coven was all present and accounted for in Raquel's attic ritual space, sitting on bright cushions that gave splashes of color to the otherwise white space. It was Halloween, the feast of Samhain, and instead of their usual journey to commune with the ancestors, tonight the coven would charge up the sigils in preparation for the working to come. They would call for more magical backup two days hence, on the Dia de los Muertos.

It was only pressure from the ancestors that had Arrow and Crescent Coven changing their longstanding plans. In the season when the ancestors were strongest, whoever ignored their messages did so at their own peril, or at the very least, at their strong discomfort. The ancestors had a way of making a witch's life miserable if they wanted to.

The sigils he, Thomas, Frater Louis, and Shekinah had worked on sat in a stack in the middle of the attic floor, surrounded by unlit beeswax tapers.

Cassiel stood, red hair flowing down her back, athame in hand, and began to mark out the quarters, using the coven's cantrip for casting.

"By earth." Pointing the double-sided blade toward the north, she drew a pentagram in the air. Then she swept the blade in an arc and pointed south. "By flame." Then on to east and west, inscribing pentagrams in each direction. "By wind. By sea."

Alejandro felt the energy build as Cassie spoke the spell. Like all magical poetry, the words' simplicity only increased the potency. Spells and prayers helped to focus the witch's will, and called all the planes of existence closer together.

She pointed her blade above and below, and then at the cross quarters. "By moon, by sun, by dusk, by dark, by witches' mark."

Alejandro felt his energy expand, deepen, and settle as Cassiel traced the edge of the circle around the space, sealing the magic. "We consecrate this holy ground, with sight, and sound, and breath twined 'round. With will and love, from below to above, let the magic portals open." Then she bowed and took her place in the circle of the coven once again.

"So mote it be," Alejandro responded with the rest of the coven.

He took in a shuddering breath, and closed his eyes for a moment.

"Ancestors, be with us," he said out loud. "We call upon you, be here now, give us aid in this time of power." Inside he added, *And don't let us fuck this up.* He leaned forward, rising slightly off his cushion, struck a match, and lit the first taper. Waving the match out, he inhaled the scent of sulfur and warming beeswax. He slid the first taper from its holder and lit the five remaining candles, waiting until each wick caught and flared before moving to the next.

"Tonight, the veils between the worlds are thin," Raquel

said. "We call upon ourselves, our ancestors, and all the powers of magic to be here now."

She clapped her hands three times, the sound a sharp retort that filled the space. The claps were something the coven had adopted from Moss's work with kami, or spirits of place. Along with words and thoughts, engaging a sound made by the body was another way to call attention to the subtler realms of being.

"These sigils are designed to protect those who need it, and offer a warning to those we want to put on alert," Alejandro said.

"We want the police to know we're watching them," Moss chimed in. "And to let the community know that someone has eyes on the police, and cares about protecting the people."

Raquel nodded at Brenda, who slid a small frame drum from one of the shelves that lined the attic knee walls. Brenda shook an errant curl from her face, and slapped out a simple rhythm, silver bracelets shaking in counterpoint to the drum.

"Breathe deeply. Draw up energy from the earth, and down from the sky," Raquel said over the drumbeat. "Draw on the power of the wheel of the year, turning around us, inside us, opening and closing doorways, defining what is possible. Think of the community. Think of the threat to the community. Focus on the sigils in the center of the circle, and let the power of the increasing night build within you, as the power of the coven builds."

Alejandro felt his consciousness sink and glide, following the cadence of Raquel's words and the slap of Brenda's hands upon the drum. His breathing slowed down so far, it felt almost as if the air in the attic was a solid, or a liquid so thick he could almost taste it.

"Draw down power, let it flow. Charge this magic, above and below. Ancestors moving, feel their power. Charge this magic, in this potent hour."

The words flowed from Brenda as if she were a channel for some other voice, drawing from some other time, or perhaps simply from the moment. Magic was tricksy that way. In the midst of the most effective rituals, a person felt outside of space and time. Alejandro felt that now, along with the current of energy humming through the room, fed by the drumming and the words.

Brenda repeated the phrase and, haltingly, the coven joined her, voices growing in certainty with each pass of the chant. It didn't take long for the chant to build in strength.

"Draw down power, let it flow. Charge this magic, above and below. Ancestors moving, feel their power. Charge this magic, in this potent hour!"

Brenda increased the pace of the drum. Alejandro swayed and moved on his cushion, rocking with the rhythm of the words.

"Draw down power, let it flow. Charge this magic, above and below. Ancestors moving, feel their power. Charge this magic, in this potent hour!"

He practically shouted the words, vocal cords straining, until, with a huge tap at the base of his skull, his spirit was free from its physical constraints. His throat relaxed, and, voice growing louder still, he chanted. As his body rocked and swayed beneath him, Alejandro floated near the attic ceiling, gazing down upon the coven, at the threads of energy twining their way toward the sigils on the floor.

Raquel raised her arms and threw back her head. The rest of the coven followed, including Alejandro's body. The magic was working. Around the room, he saw the shadows of

the ancestors, more and more gathering each minute. It seemed that they were pleased. He floated back into his body, snapping into place just as Brenda changed the rhythm again. Raquel started clapping. His palms tingled with each smack.

"Draw down power, let it flow. Charge this magic, above and below. Ancestors moving, feel their power. Charge this magic, in this potent hour!"

The magic built and built inside the attic room. The coven's voices were loud, ringing in his ears, and ringing past the veils of the year, calling the ancestors, calling the magic, calling the powers.

The chant went on and on. The pressure built inside him once again. And new words came, calling for him to weave them above and within the magic chant.

"Ancestors, be with us now! Ancient ones, come down! Ancestors, be with us now! Ancient ones, come down!" Moss and Selene's voice joined his, rising and falling in counterpoint to the other chant.

The drum kicked up another notch and Alejandro began to vibrate. It was almost too much. He felt as if he'd shake out of his skin.

Raquel and Brenda started chanting wordless tones, weaving, weaving, weaving the spell. The ancestors moved in a ring around the room. The power built, higher and higher, deeper and deeper. Alejandro felt as if his spirit and body might snap, and then, with a mighty roar, Raquel cocked her fingers as if about to throw a dart into the center of the room.

A dart of magical power. A dart aimed at the heart of the sigils. Every person in the coven did the same. He felt the fingers of his right hand cock back.

"Ahhhhhhhhhhhhhhhhh!" Their voices rose in a mighty

crescendo, Raquel's hand snapped forward, seconds later so did his.

The dart of energy smacked into the sigils, fluttering the stack of papers.

The voices stopped. The drum stopped. The only sound was the panting of exertion, and a soft moan.

The moan came from his mouth. Alejandro's eyes rolled back in his head and, pitching toward the candles in the center, he collapsed.

40

SHEKINAH

"You passed out, knocked over a bunch of candles, and...and now you're going out on the streets at night to engage in illegal activity? I can't *believe* you! Can't someone else put up fliers? You need to rest for the big working coming up. Don't you?"

She was ready to fling her phone into the street, and was aware of Tish beside her, acting as if she wasn't at all interested in the heated conversation.

Alejandro's voice was placating, trying to reassure her. But, much as the words made sense, that this needed to be done right now—tonight—she couldn't see why he had to be the one to do it.

"No. We'll talk about it later. Just...stay safe out there, okay? If you get hurt and mess up the *big ritual you have to do in two more nights*, I'll be even more pissed, and you won't forgive yourself."

She hung up the phone, scowl on her face. She couldn't *believe* him. Oh, he tried to convince her that it was just putting up flyers, no big deal, but she knew better. And after five years of relationship, she also knew better than to do more than register a complaint and pass along her concern.

"You can't control your partner," she reminded herself.

"What's up?" Tish asked. They were standing on the street in front of the Shiva Center. After spending an hour or so in the park with the families, they had grabbed some food. Over dinner, it came to Shekinah in a flash: she knew what her next step was. She needed to try. To see if they could use chanting to help these people.

Maybe tonight, Halloween, could be a trial run. She needed to see if people—Yogi Basu in particular, but others at the Center—would be willing to do the work at all, and then do it again to back up the witches on Dia de los Muertos.

Tish was along to provide moral support, and because, as she'd told Shekinah, she wasn't ready to go home and try to get to sleep. She was too afraid the dreams and visions would come back when she was alone.

Shekinah didn't know what to do about that. If it weren't for the news that her partner had collapsed that evening, she would have immediately offered to spend the night at Tish's and keep watch. But now it seemed she might have two people who needed tending. Shekinah sighed, then realized Tish was waiting for an answer.

"Oh, just my lover being stupid." She shrugged. "What can you do?"

Tish smiled. "In my experience? Absolutely nothing."

Both women laughed, then Tish said grew serious again.

"Well, if you're going to do this, you better get in there. Class starts in fifteen minutes."

Shekinah nodded, shook out her hands, straightened her spine, and headed up the walkway towards the door. The windows on either side glowed with light, and she could practically feel the waves of energy rolling out of the building. Or maybe that was just her, responding to the fact that she was about to enter her spiritual home, and see her teacher, and the kundalini serpents were activated.

Her heart pounded and her mouth was dry, but despite the fear, she was also filled with certainty. Maybe that was another way the two serpents worked, bringing opposites together in one place. Certainty and fear could coexist within her. Both carried their own energy, and neither one had to suppress the other. Now if she could only figure out how to harness them both.

She pulled open the heavy Craftsman door and allowed Tish to head in first, before following her friend into a bustle of activity. People taking off coats and shoes and talking. A quiet burst of laughter came from the dressing room down the hall. Yogi Basu walked towards them, beaming with a huge smile.

"Shekinah! And Tish! You didn't say anything about coming by tonight!" His dark eyes sought out Shekinah's, holding layer upon layer of questions that seemed to pierce her soul.

Shekinah glanced away, down at the smooth oak wood floor, then flexed her toes inside of her shoes and rocked forward and back slightly. Testing her equilibrium. Trying to stand tall, to call upon the twin serpents, praying for the activation of their power.

She cleared her throat and returned her eyes to Yogi Basu's steady gaze. "Do you still want me to take teacher training?"

He nodded. "Yes?" The question hung in the air. Waiting. Waiting for her to say something. To claim something.

No time like the present.

"I've studied with you for ten years. I've watched you

teach. I've practiced and I've prayed. And I'm ready. I am willing to take the training, but..." She cleared her throat and spread both feet flat on the floor. "I'm also willing and ready to teach. And I wonder if you'll give me a chance tonight. I want to try something new."

Yogi Basu stroked his beard, paying no attention to the people moving around them. Paying no attention to the fact that the clock ticked and the practice space was filling up.

"You want to take a risk?" he finally said. "And you want Shiva Center to take a risk?"

Shekinah knew he understood. He was her teacher after all. Her surrogate parent. The one who tried his best for her. The one who gave his life force to all of his students, connecting them to a lineage as old as time itself. Of course, he understood. And she didn't know if she found that frightening, or exhilarating.

"Yes." She put every bit of kundalini energy that she could into that one word. Then she swallowed and said it again. "Yes. I want us to take that risk."

Yogi Basu said nothing. Time stretched, and the air around them grew thick with power and possibility. Shekinah noticed that the hallway was empty. Quiet. All of the yogis were ready, waiting for class to begin.

With a sideways bow, Yogi Basu swept out an arm, gesturing toward the open pocket doors leading to the practice and meditation hall.

"Thank you." She bowed back at her teacher, then she and Tish slipped off their coats and shoes. Rising once more, Tish gave her arm a reassuring squeeze. Then they walked past their teacher, into the practice hall.

Shekinah just hoped this worked.

41

ALEJANDRO

Standing on the street, unable to even pace, Alejandro really didn't know what to say to Shekinah. There was no rational explanation for his actions, just this fire and buzz at the base of his skull, the ancestors pushing him on, despite his headache and dodgy stomach. Earbuds in, he tried hard to not sigh. She would hear that, and it would only make matters worse.

The night air was cool and tall elms filtered the street lights, making the Northeast Portland residential street seem almost suburban, despite the fact that he could still hear traffic from MLK, just four blocks away. The neighborhood was a mix of houses and light industrial, peppered with brand new condos like the one he lived in, not so far away.

He felt Moss and his comrades waiting. Oh, Moss was patient enough, but he could tell the others were wondering what the fuck was going on.

"Yes. Talk later. I love you." But she'd already hung up by the time he said those last three words. Yeah. She was pissed.

Alejandro, hands trembling, popped his earbuds out and stored them in their little hard case, shoving them and his phone into his jeans. He still felt woozy from collapsing after charging up the sigils, which meant Shekinah's worry and annoyance were well founded. Not that he was going to admit that to anyone. Not now, at least. Not until this whole working was done.

"You ready?" Moss asked.

"Give me a minute. Sorry."

He took a moment to try and re-center himself and slow the trembling queasiness down. It wasn't quite working, but after a few breaths he at least felt a little bit better. Sending a breath out to the edge of his aura, he imagined the protections he had embedded in his energy field activating. If that piece of magic wasn't just wishful thinking, hopefully it would help, too.

Not too long ago, he would have been certain of his magic and his practice. These days, though? Midlife crisis was a bitch.

The small group scuffing the sidewalk with their high-top sneakers was gathered on one of the side streets a few blocks away from the main drag of MLK, and four more blocks south of the North Precinct. They all wore hooded sweatshirts like his, and two of them had backpacks that carried the fliers, staplers, and extra rolls of tape. The hoodies were precautions against cameras, and Moss had told him that his usual snazzy suede motorcycle style jacket was way too conspicuous anyway. So a Timbers hoodie it was. Turned out that a lot of local activists were rabid members of the Timbers Army, a sort of soccer fan club. Who knew that it had an anti-fascist wing?

Even when it felt like shit, the world was a strange and wonderful place. He wondered if he'd felt that way as

Alejandro Juan, too, before he was dragged to death. He swallowed down the sour, metallic taste at the back of his mouth and fished in his jean's pocket for some gum. Nothing. The gum was in his jacket, left in one of the cars.

"Alejandro?" Moss's voice was quiet, but had acquired an edge.

No more stalling. Alejandro pulled up his hood and nodded. Moss's housemate Tariq led the way. Alejandro and the rest of the crew fast walked behind his lanky, loose-limbed stride, sneakers smacking softly on the concrete. No boots tonight. Tariq's orders. All Alejandro had were Nikes to go with his fancy jeans, but he wasn't trying to win any activist fashion contests, right?

As they approached the first telephone pole, Moss turned to him. "Want to hang the first one?"

He nodded and grabbed the outstretched stapler. Sending a quick breath across the sigil for protection, he saw it flare in his mind's eye. *Thwack! Thwack! Thwack! Thwack!* The staples shooting home into the ragged, tarry wood sounded so loud. No one seemed concerned though, so it must have just been him.

The quartered square with a circle inside looked good, strong, lit by a nearby streetlight. The words "STRONGER TOGETHER" sent a message to the neighborhood, boosted by the magic.

Every group out tonight had at least one witch with them, able to give the sigils an extra boost. They were spread out across the city, heading all the way into Gresham in the east and Beaverton to the west. Alejandro and Moss's group had already hit North Portland proper, and were now at the start of northeast. Right near the North Precinct of the Portland Police Bureau. Heading toward a lot of surveillance cameras.

Despite having done several actions with the coven, especially over the past year, Alejandro was nervous. He usually preferred to work on political and social change from behind his computer, or by changing the balance of power in boardrooms. Now that he knew more about Alejandro Juan, he wondered if there was a reason he leaned a little more conservative than folks like Tariq and Moss. He had literally been tortured to death by police.

"Hey, man, you don't have to do this." Tariq stood beside him, one hand on his shoulder, concern on his face, half hidden in the shadow thrown by the soft black hood that hid his hair. Had Alejandro stopped? He didn't remember. "You can go back to the car. Wait this out."

The base of Alejandro's skull flared, sending a small strobe of pain toward his temples.

"No. I'll keep up. Sorry about that."

Tariq nodded and turned to head off again. Moss stood a few feet away, watching, but the rest of the crew was busy stapling sigils to phone poles or taping them to fences.

"Hey, Tariq?" He kept his voice soft. It wouldn't do to have names carry out here in the half dark. The taller man paused and turned. "Keep an eye on me though. Okay?"

Tariq just nodded and loped off to join the rest of the squad.

They were rounding the corner, heading toward the Boys and Girls Club, where they planned to post several "Stronger Together" sigils out front.

The North Precinct stood across from the club. With its red, curved awning facing a small parking lot, the police station looked like a flooring tile warehouse or something. Not a place where people worked to patrol the formerly mostly Black neighborhood, deciding what random dark-skinned person looked like they must be in a gang.

They taped a few sigils to the Boys and Girls Club fence, making sure to keep heads down, faces well out of the range of security cameras. He had to admire Moss and Tariq's crew. They were quick, quiet, and efficient, and didn't get in each other's way. He quickly decided he was a liability in the work and backed off from hanging the fliers.

Instead, he and Moss tag-teamed giving the sigils some extra oomph once they were hung. Just a flash of witchy fire, sent with a thought and a crooked finger.

Tariq and the others had moved across the street, on the blank, broad side of the police station. One person would roll out and cut tape while the other held the sigil to post, fence, or wall. They must have decided staplers were too loud for this part of the operation. Moss moved to do his part, when Alejandro realized Tariq and his partner were no longer visible.

They must have gone around the front of the station.

"Shit."

Shouting and sounds of a scuffle came from around the corner. Alejandro didn't think. Just ran, barreling around the side of the hulking building, heading directly toward what looked like a small scrum.

A cop had hold of one of Tariq's arms, and was shouting for backup. The other activist tugged Tariq the other direction. Both activists strained against the cop.

Alejandro held out both arms and ran straight into Tariq. Smacking his hands around a slender waist, he just kept running, felt a yank, felt Tariq stumble and then catch his feet.

Then they were all on the run.

Alejandro didn't stop to see what the cops were doing. He ran as hard and fast as his pounding head would let him.

One of the other comrades, a small woman, grabbed his hand and pulled, helping him along.

Ancestors, help me, he prayed, then put on a burst of speed.

Block after block they ran, deeper into the neighborhood, away from the brightly lit main streets. One of their crew cheated down an alleyway, and everyone pounded after.

Even though his head was about to split open, and he wanted to puke, Alejandro realized he also felt a barely familiar sensation, burbling up inside of him like the beginnings of laughter.

For the first time in years, he felt free.

42

SHEKINAH

Shekinah was sweating.

The white-clad group in front of her was, too. Sweat glistened on faces and clothing darkened as moisture ran down their bodies.

"Ek Ongkar Sat Nam Siri Wahe Guroo..." Infinite Creator. Name of Truth. Ultimate Wisdom.

They had chanted for twenty minutes now, and the energy showed no sign of abating. In fact, it built and built. It felt as though if she reached out, she could tug the air around her like a shawl.

"Ek Ongkar Sat Nam Siri Wahe Guroo!" Their bodies snapped and twisted, side to side. There was power in truth. There was power in prayer. Together, maybe, just maybe, the scales would fall from their hearts and eyes, and the truth would be revealed.

Tish prayed with fierce zeal, eyes filled with fire.

The kundalini serpents rose and twined, rose and twined.

"Ek Ongkar Sat Nam!"

Voices bellowed, louder and louder, as the energy rose,

stronger and stronger building in the room until every person was taut as a quivering wire.

"Siri Wahe Guroo!"

Shekinah raised her arms, then clapped her hands together, a sharp retort that pierced the energies like an arrow.

Arms fell to sides. The twisting and snapping stopped. The only sounds in the room were soft pants, as people tried to regulate their breathing.

"May the truth be told, over and over," Shekinah said. "May the truth be revealed. May a juggernaut roll through, carrying the power of all who have gone before."

"Jai, Jagganath!" Tish called out.

"Jai, Jagganath!" the rest of the class said in response.

"Jai, Shiva!" Shekinah called.

"Jai, Shiva!"

"May there be justice, in this world, here and now. May we be instruments of your justice. May we be unafraid of battle. Lord Shiva, keep us strong, that we may enact the work of truth. May we speak clearly, live simply, fight with love in our hearts and strength in our minds."

As Shekinah finished her prayer, she opened her eyes, only to find half the room with eyes still closed in rapture, and the other half staring at her with wide eyes.

Yogi Basu entered the room.

Walking quietly, with steady gait, he approached Shekinah, who bowed. He stood beside her.

"Our sister Shekinah has asked a great thing of us tonight. She has asked us to look beyond our simple school. To look outward, more deeply at the world. And she is right to do so. The Lord of Truth wears many faces and holds many weapons. What weapon do you wield? What courage do you need? There are people in pain everywhere, and yes, some of them are in this room, and yes, our practice helps to ease suffering. But our sister Shekinah thinks that we can do more."

Everyone was staring, which would have made Shekinah wither, just a few months ago. But he was right to ask her to train. People could look at her, and she didn't have to crumble. She didn't need to pretend to be less than she was.

Her life was her truth.

Yogi Basu turned to her. "Shekinah? Is there more that you would tell us?"

She swallowed, then tilted her chin up and lengthened her spine.

"The police have declared war on the most vulnerable in our communities and it is time we started doing more. If Shiva Center is to truly be a sanctuary, we must do more than simply feed the poor once a month or so. We must welcome immigrants. We must open our hearts to grieving families. We must tell the city of Portland that enough is enough. No more killing. No more lies."

The words stopped at the edges of her lips. Had she said too much?

Tish looked steadily at her, fierce look still on her face. Yogi Basu gestured for her to continue.

She looked around the room. Everyone was perfectly still, in that way that only practitioners of some deep form of meditation or physical practice—or sometimes the most skilled master craftspeople—seemed able to achieve. The energy of the kundalini serpents was still palpable in the room, and she swore she smelled datura, though the night blooming flower grew nowhere in the neighborhood.

Lord Shiva... She didn't need to finish the prayer. She had just prayed for one solid hour, the last half hour shouting out the name of Truth.

"Today, Tish and I sat with the families of people killed by the Portland Police Bureau. Our sister Tish has been having terrible visions of more killings yet to come. I want us to use our spiritual power to help stop her visions from coming true. Tish?"

Tish gave one quick nod, then stepped to the front of the room, standing at Shekinah's side, between her and Yogi Basu.

"I have had dreams and visions of my brother, lying before me, dead on the ground. And others have been having visions, too. Of strange rituals. A powerful, spiritual force working for what I can only call evil. And here we are, raising a spiritual force of our own." She gazed at every person in turn. "So what Shekinah and I are asking, with Yogi Basu's permission, is for us to channel that spiritual force to counter the terrible power of the police. I know it is a lot to ask, and not what we usually do, but..."

Yogi Basu held up a hand to stop Tish from saying more.

"Enough, sister," he said, voice filled with compassion. "Their hearts and minds can decide what is too much. Shekinah?"

Tears were close to the surface now, but when she spoke, her voice was calm and clear. "Two evenings from now, on November second, we are asking you to pray with all your power, that truth be seen and justice rise like a beacon in the darkness. We ask that you let yourself be illuminated with this fire, and send it out, to fill the city with warmth and light."

One of the men in the back of the room cleared his throat and spoke.

"With your permission, I would like to speak."

Here it comes.... Shekinah thought. The railing against dragging their spiritual practice into politics.

Shekinah and Tish both glanced toward Yogi Basu, who simply gestured for the man to continue.

"Will you be leading us in prayer again, like tonight? Or should we do this on our own?"

"I will be leading you myself," Yogi Basu replied. "I believe that Shekinah and Tish have other work to do that night. Am I correct?"

The tears she'd been holding back filled her eyes.

"Yes, Yogi. We will be with others, trying to hold back this force."

"Then it is so," he said. "Whoever wishes to help? Come pray. We will do our work as our sisters do theirs. But it is all the same work, yes? It is all the same prayer."

Shekinah bowed to the group assembled before her, then turned to bow at Tish. And, bending even lower still, she bowed to her teacher, then bent all the way to the floor to touch his lotus feet.

43

ALEJANDRO

He wasn't ready. He would never be ready. When he'd complained about it to Brenda and Raquel, Raquel had simply raised an eyebrow and Brenda replied, "Like the rest of us, you've been preparing for this your whole life. And as a matter of fact, it looks like you've been preparing for several lifetimes, haven't you?"

He had no response to that, and had simply headed past the purple Celtic knot work curtain that led to the back room of Brenda's shop, carrying photos of his grandparents and Alejandro Juan for the altar. His athamé was sheathed in his pocket.

His ancestors had wanted the ritual to be in front of his living room ofrenda, but he'd explained there just wasn't room. Too many people planned to attend. The ancestors had agreed to send representatives, instead. Hence the three photos.

Brenda had gotten a rug for the room at least. The large, emerald-toned rug was also bordered with a running knot pattern. It made the room feel less...clinical than it had in the past.

Tempest and Lucy plopped cushions around the edges of the rug as Tobias set up four candles in the cardinal colors in the center on a round wooden tray, along with a thurible for incense and a large blue chalice. Lucy looked good, strong and hale, but yeah, Tempest definitely didn't look well.

"Terra and her crew made up the fliers asking folks to pray to their ancestors to protect our communities from the police." Moss's voice startled Alejandro. He gave his coven mate a sideways hug that Moss returned, though he didn't stop speaking. "English and Spanish. She already dropped them at the Mercado and a few other Latinx-owned places around town. She said folks seemed receptive."

Alejandro breathed a sigh of relief and felt the ancestors buzzing in response. "It's good to know it's not just my ancestors who'll be working overtime tonight. Thank Terra for me?"

"Will do." Moss moved off to help with chairs and cushions.

Juggling the photos into one hand, Alejandro drew his athamé out of its sheath and walked toward the central altar tray. He'd hesitated between his wand and the blade, before figuring the blade felt more useful for tonight's purposes. Protection and attack. But now he regretted leaving his wand behind. He wanted both magical tools tonight, though he could not have rationally explained why. Sometimes objects had a mind of their own.

He crouched down and added his double-edged knife to the altar, then carefully placed the photos between the candles.

"Hey, brother."

"Hey, yourself." Tobias swept a dark lock of hair from his forehead and leaned over to embrace Alejandro. He smelled medicinal, as if the herbs he worked with had soaked into his skin. Pulling back, Tobias gave him a quick kiss on the lips, then looked into his eyes.

"You got this. *We've* got this."

"I hope so. It's just all so strange. This ancestor shit. The fact that it's me this time... I'm used to the rest of you living these magically charged lives, you know, and I'm just the ordinary, bourgeois IT guy who cheers you on."

"Oh, bullshit."

Alejandro shrugged. It sure felt that way, but no matter. "But also, we're doing all this work on the astral, figuring the cops are doing some sort of ritual, too. We have no idea of the timing, other than it feels like things are coming to a head. In the past, we've always either had a solid outside event to focus on, whether or not we've pushed the timing. And we haven't included the community on this one, either, which doesn't quite feel right."

"We haven't?" Tobias asked, then gestured around the room, which had filled up as they conferred.

Alejandro looked up. There was Thomas. Seeing him made Alejandro's heart thump in his chest. If he hadn't also been so nervous, he was sure he'd be having a different sort of response, too. Next to him was Frater Louis. Then Moss, Tariq, Terra, Barbara Jean, and some other members of the anarchist crew. Alejandro would have to ask later how the hell Moss had convinced them to be part of a strictly magical operation. Tobias's boyfriend, Aiden, a Catholic Worker who helped run one of the local soup kitchens was there, along with two other people Alejandro vaguely recognized.

"Your Catholic boyfriend is here?"

Now it was Tobias's turn to shrug. "He knows it's important. And he trusts us by now."

Fellow programmer Olivia walked in, holding the curtain for her girlfriend, Grace, to roll through. Olivia nodded at Alejandro as they found a spot in the corner of the room near Lucy.

A couple of heathens had shown up. Alejandro remembered them from the battle against the so-called Patriots at the waterfront park just after Beltane. One of them, a burly white guy with a big brown beard, gave him a small wave. The witches from the shop down in Salem were there, too. Shani and Lindy.

Damn. The coven had been busy the past couple of days while Alejandro worked with Shekinah, Tish, Brenda, and Raquel, trying to get tonight's ritual together.

Maybe Tobias was right. This was as strong a cross section of community as they'd ever had.

Then Shekinah walked through the curtain.

"Thanks, Tobias." He squeezed his coven brother's shoulder and rose to greet her with a kiss.

44
——

SHEKINAH

The room was packed. She hadn't expected so many people to show up for whatever this weird ritual was going to end up being.

And then her lover was heading across the room, face intent, walking across the big green rug, straight at her. He had worried her plenty the past couple of days, but there had been no time to dwell on it. They had work to do. Everything else would have to wait until they were through this.

"Hey," he said softly, brown eyes warm, his face still the beautiful one that had drawn her in. He slipped his hands into hers, interlacing their fingers, and then he kissed her. Gently. Their lips met in a promise that they were still in this together, and would be for as long as love remained.

"Hey yourself," she said when they pulled apart, hands still interlaced. "You doing okay? Ready?"

"Not really, but both Brenda and Raquel insisted that I had to do this even if I wasn't ready."

They both laughed at that, though there was more affection than humor in the sound.

She looked around the room then, scanning the faces

both familiar and those she hadn't yet met. One was missing.

"Tish isn't here yet?"

The curtain rattled behind Shekinah and, as if she heard her name, Tish burst through.

"Hey! I meant to get here earlier, but I was meeting with Jeremy Landis's mother and it was hard to get away. The grief...I can't even imagine having your child killed like that. When I told her what we were doing though, she gave me this." Tish held out her hand. Resting in her palm was a gold cross. It looked like a lapel pin.

"She said he used to wear this to church when he ushered. She wanted us to use it tonight, in whatever way we needed to. And when I told her about Yogi Basu leading chanting tonight, she said she'd contact her church phone tree and get a prayer rope going, too."

"Wow," Shekinah said. "That's fantastic." She blinked her eyes against threatening tears—again. When in the world had she become such a crier?

"This may be the most interfaith ritual we've ever done," Alejandro chimed in. "Hey, babe, I'm gonna go say hi to Thomas. Okay?"

Raising a hand to his face, she felt the soft prickle of his pointed beard against her skin. He was a dashing man, her love, despite the tired fear that still haunted his eyes. "Of course."

Tish shook her head. "I still don't know how you guys do it, but I'm glad it works for you, you know? Maybe I'll find someone one day."

"Once this is over, let's work on it. Okay?"

Brenda and Raquel came through the curtain then.

"It's almost showtime," Raquel said. "Tish, you let me

know if you need anything. Anything at all, at any time. You got me?"

"I got you."

"Okay," she said. "You, too, Shekinah. Brenda and Tobias will be monitoring Alejandro, and Tempest and I will be looking after both of you. We don't want any casualties tonight."

Raquel moved past them then, heading toward Tobias.

"Do either of you have any questions?" Brenda asked. She smelled of tuberose and rain. The scents felt comforting. Clean. Shekinah inhaled deeply, letting the perfume clear the cobwebs from her head.

"I don't think so," Tish replied.

Shekinah shook her head. If she started asking questions, she'd never stop. She had to trust the certainty she'd felt while chanting two nights before. She had to trust Yogi Basu, the coven, and everyone else.

Besides, she wasn't the one with the high stakes, was she? That would be people like Tish and her brother. Or the families she'd met in the park.

All she could do was show up and do her best to help make things right.

45

ALEJANDRO

Cassiel cast the circle. Eyes half closed, part of the ragged circle of bodies staggered two deep, Alejandro could almost see the flickering of ætheric blue fire as it moved from quarter to quarter. Cassie, red hair an unbound flame down her back, spoke the holy words of conjuring. Earth and wind. Flame and sea. And all the powers above, below, beyond and in between. He let the cadence of the familiar cantrip wash over and through him, breathing deeply, slowly, becoming more and more present as priest. As witch.

The air smelled slightly of ozone, and the mingled scents of Thomas and Shekinah. He sat in between old and new, past and future. He only hoped that he could actually do something in the present. It felt as if too much was riding on tonight's ritual, but that, of course, was the very reason it needed to be done.

Cassiel's milk-pale wrists and hands carved through the air, her double-sided blade trailing the blue mist that now formed a dome around the room.

"With will and love, from below to above, let the magic

portals open." She stood in the center of the room, arms crossed over her chest, and bowed.

"So mote it be," the witches in the room replied.

And then it was his turn. He squeezed Shekinah and Thomas's hands and stepped forward, beckoning to Tish, who stood on the other side of the room, flanked by Brenda and Raquel. They both moved to the center of the room. Alejandro looked around, vision still soft, calling on the vision of this world and the ætheric realms. He saw the glimmering of candlelight on Brenda and Selene's moonstone pendants, and from the silver of Frater Louis's unicursal hexagram that hung from a gold chain against the black of his shirt. Tobias and Tempest both wore silver pentacles, and Raquel wore a bright necklace of heavy blue glass beads.

All of these symbols were arrayed against the forces they would fight tonight. He touched his own pentagram, which he rarely wore, but he'd spent some time last night charging it up and it had sat on his ofrenda all night. After that, he and Shekinah had made love, before he dropped into blessedly dreamless sleep.

He breathed in all of it, drawing on the hope he felt in the strength of those assembled, and drawing on his own practice, and the prayers and practices of all the ancestors who had come before him.

"Ancestors, we call to you! We stand here, as an army of magic and love, to lend our power to the work of justice." His words rippled through the æthers, sending out the call.

"Ancestors," Tish called, "we honor you! Though we come from different backgrounds and traditions, we ask that those of you who wish to help us with this work of justice join us here tonight. We need you."

"Ancestors of spirit and of blood, we ask you to bring

your power to this work that has been done for so many years. We are but one small strand in a mighty thread woven by those who have come before us. Let us be a bridge that leads toward justice, founded upon the law of love." Alejandro's vocal chords strained, trying to hold back the burst of energy that tried to take over his body.

Stop fighting, hermano. Let me in. Let us become who we really are.

"Love is the law, love under will!" Frater Louis and Thomas said.

"My law is love unto all beings!" shouted Brenda.

Alejandro's energy flared, and he saw his twin step out from his body and turn. As he looked into his own dark eyes, Alejandro fell. He dimly heard some shouting, and felt hands on his body, easing him onto some sort of soft carpeting. Smelled familiar scents of people who loved him.

And then that was all gone.

His bones ground into hard earth and his joints screamed from strain.

Clouds gathered overhead. Past the distant mountains, thunder rumbled. The afternoon darkened with the coming of dusk and the gathering storm.

The air was thick and the pressure of the storm built inside his head. Alejandro tasted the grit of dirt. The semiarid Oregon desert was no joke. He just hoped the storm didn't wash too much soil away. Or drown him. But maybe it would put a damper on the preparations for the giant bonfire the pendejos seemed to be building. He was trussed up like one of his cattle for what must have been an hour as the lawmen stacked and clattered wood and branches in the center of a big circle. The edges of the space were defined by iron brackets that would hold torches come full night.

He really did not want to be present for whatever was

going to happen when darkness fell. He needed to get the fuck away, but every movement further tightened the bonds around his ankles and wrists.

The stink of human sweat and chewing tobacco hit him just before Sheriff Carlson stepped into his view. The man bent to peer at him, and the tin star pinned to the tanned brown leather of his jacket shone dully in the gray light.

Alejandro knew it would gleam brightly once the fires were lit.

"You gonna tell us where your daddy's gold is buried? If you do, we'll slit your throat before throwing your sorry ass on the fire. 'Cause we're what passes for gentlemen around here, and unlike you heathens, a gentleman always offer a coup de grace."

Alejandro remained silent. He'd learned years ago that talking meant little to these ranchers who fancied themselves to be the law.

"If you don't? That might just mean you get dragged first. Softened up, as it were. We got some horses that just love to drag a man."

Alejandro gazed up at the broad face, tanned and wrinkled. He'd never hated a man's face more in his life. He worked at the grit in his mouth, trying to work up some spit in answer.

Carlson's right foot shot out and the solid tip of his boot thumped into Alejandro's gut. A huff of breath was all the noise he would make, though the pain felt like fire.

He wished like hell he had his granny's brujería. He would curse this man—curse all of these men—to whatever hell they most feared.

46

SHEKINAH

Alejandro just...collapsed. Raquel and Tobias rushed toward him, catching him before he crashed into the central candles, and eased him down onto the rug. Shekinah's heart flew upward, half choking off her breath. She started forward, but Brenda grabbed her wrist. When had the witch moved to her part of the circle?

Alejandro's eyes flickered behind his lids and he moaned, then hissed sharply, as if he was in pain.

"Is he going to be all right?" she asked Brenda.

"He's Raquel and Tobias's job, not yours. Focus on your own work. The work you were brought here to do. And if you can't do that? Focus on your friend, Tish."

Tish rocked and swayed on her feet, but seemed okay, and the witch with short white hair—Tempest—stood at her side, one hand up behind Tish's back, clearly ready to help her. Her opposite, a tall non-binary-looking Goth named Selene stood on Tish's other side. Clearly her friend was well in hand. Brenda was right. Shekinah had a lot of people counting on her, and her job was to pray, not to get sucked out of herself by useless worry.

But frankly, she found it hard to focus. Everywhere she turned, something was happening, and people were doing strange things.

Besides Tish and Alejandro, there were the anarchists. They formed a smaller circle in the southern quadrant of the room, crouched around the sigils. They were doing something with Frater Louis and Thomas.

She glanced down at the central altar, eye caught by the small gold cross on the black lacquered tray. The four candles around it gleamed softly, casting red, green, blue, and gold light that bounced up off the black tray, reflecting the colors in the banners on the room's four walls.

The cross was a reminder. There were a bunch of Catholics lending their prayers to the working right now, and Brenda was right, that's what Shekinah was supposed to be doing, too. Calling upon Lord Shiva to protect Tish on her journey.

From the back pocket of her jeans, she drew out the one object that had called to come to the ritual. It was a gold compact mirror that had belonged to her great-grandmother. When she slipped it into her pocket before leaving the house, she had no idea what she would use it for. All she knew was that Raquel had instructed everyone to bring something that reminded or connected them to their ancestors.

But now she knew exactly what the mirror was for. Besides connecting her to Grandmother Rachel, it was a clear mirror, unmarked even by its age. Its reflection was true. She snapped open the clasp and looked at herself. In the light of the colored candles, she could have been any age, and from any time. She supposed that was good. Nodding at her reflection, she felt the weight of the gold compact in her right hand. She touched the forefinger and thumb of her left hand together, and raised her hand in the mudrā of truth.

"Om Namah Shivaya," she chanted softly. "Protect us all. Help us to reflect the truth. Om Namah Shivaya. Om Namah Shivaya."

Touching the tip of her tongue to the roof of her mouth, she let the chanting go for a moment, and tuned in to her breath.

47

ALEJANDRO

"Alejandro. Brother. Come back to us. We need you."

"What's happening to him?"

Voices. A familiar warmth. Head pounding. Gut roiling. Light. Fire. The metallic taste of fear.

"Alejandro, bridge the past with the future. Be a priest. Find Tish."

Priest? What did that mean?

Hoofbeats. Pounding. Dragged across hard ground. So. Much. Pain.

A strong, warm hand on his forehead.

Then his spirit was flying, yanked from one world and hurtling toward the next. He almost blacked out from the vertigo, swallowed hard, willing himself to not hurl.

Can I even throw up on the astral planes? The thought was fleeting, but it belonged to Alejandro Guillermo, not Alejandro Juan. Far below, in that room in Brenda's shop, he felt his body inhale. Exhale. Felt the hands working the edges of his ætheric body, soothing away the pain and sense of illness and terror.

He sought out Tish's signature, seeking out that sense of

strength and love, of solidity and purpose, of a vulnerability and fear buried just beneath the surface.

The bonfire and horses felt far below, behind him somewhere, though a strong cord still connected him to that space. To his torture. Anger sliced through his belly and he felt his friends, his coven, his lovers, his community, all feeding the work. *We got this.*

48

SHEKINAH

She felt the serpents twine up her body, mirroring each other, and somehow—she just knew it—mirroring the energy rising from her lover's aura, which alternated deep blue and a gold as bright as day.

You don't need to know what that means. Just pray. Was that her own inner voice, or the voice of her teacher? That didn't matter either.

Each inhalation drew the cosmic energies upward. Each exhalation sent them fountaining from her head. As the kundalini built inside her, she felt the energy rise everywhere in the room, and beyond the room. There were worlds upon worlds, all present, and the work must be done in and through them all.

Her body began to move in prayer, almost of its own accord. Her head snapped right, to the mirror, and then left, to the mudrā of truth. The chant that had anchored Shekinah to her practice all these years rose in her throat and spilled out from her mouth.

"Sa Ray Sa Sa, Sa Ray Sa Sa, Sa Ray Sa Sa, Sa Rang..." Infinite Reality. Infinite Presence.

The chant began slowly, softly, then built in power. The tempo increased, and her body moved around her center, fed by the serpents twining at her core. She was one with the Infinite. Piercing the shadows. Reflecting light.

49

ALEJANDRO

The threads of past, present, and future were all wound in and around him. It was through these threads that he saw Tish, standing on the astral planes, holding a flaming sword like some avenging angel. The Sword of Enlightenment that could sever the heads of believers and non-believers alike.

She was surrounded by cops.

Alejandro barreled into the center of the circle and placed his back against hers, athame in one hand, wand in the other. *Where did that come from?* But he knew. Same place as Tish's sword. Tools had a way of appearing on the astral when the magic worker most needed them.

::*How do you want to play this?*:: he asked.

::*I want to take every one of these fuckers down,*:: she replied. ::*But we've got to figure out if that will take care of whatever egregore they've built or not.*::

He and Tish circled slowly, Tish waving the flaming sword in a figure eight. He held his blade and wand loosely crossed over his chest, muscles flexed, ready to strike in an instant.

As they circled, Alejandro scanned, seeking out the nexus of power. It was within none of the men or women standing there, sneering and clacking their teeth as if they wanted to bite. He shoved down his discomfort at the image —things on the astral tended to show the layers beneath, and they were often horrifying if not simply strange.

And there he was. The new chief. The one Moss had talked about. The new sheriff in town, as it were.

Fuck if it wasn't Sheriff Carlson. The man wore a different face, but his astral signature was the same. He smelled so strongly of chewing tobacco and sweat, Alejandro could almost taste it.

Alejandro Guillermo felt Alejandro Juan stir inside him.

::*What shall we do?*:: He wasn't sure who he was asking. Which of his selves. Or Tish?

::*Do as the lady says, and take these pendejos down. Ruin them and sever their ties to earth so they cannot make this evil magic again. Salt the earth on which they stand. Let nothing root or grow.*::

He felt the rightness of the words, and felt assent from Tish.

Okay. They knew what they were going to do. Now they just needed to figure out how.

50

SHEKINAH

"Ra Ma Da Sa Sa Say So Hung!"

Her prayers were full-throated now, unfettered. Her voice was strong with the power of He Who Danced in Love and War. The mirror winked and flashed with light.

It was all going to be all right. She could feel it now. Every cluster of the room played its part, and each part worked with the larger whole. She could also feel the force they were arrayed against. The old magic blended with the new. A magic of force and suppression, a magic of oppression and control. A magic that had been seeded thousands of years before and was coming to fruition in this time.

It had needed twin serpents of its own to come together, binding and unbinding.

"Ra Ma Da Sa Sa Say So Hung..." The Sun and the Moon twined with the Infinite, sending healing to those who were in need.

Weaving in and around her chanting, other prayers rose and fell and rose again, forming a palpable web of power.

She saw six-pointed stars. Five-pointed stars. Flashes of light. Ambition and greed. And moving among it all, were twin powers. Earth and air. Past and future. Love and war. The power of each ebbed and flowed. But somehow, somewhere, truth showed its face in all. The Infinite rang true, beyond time.

"Ra Ma Da Sa Sa Say So Hung!" Shekinah screamed out the words. Sweat ran down her face. The mirror shone. Her arm was raised, hand in the mudrā of truth. She was dimly aware of physical pain. It didn't matter. The only thing that mattered was that she pray.

In front of her, two dark eyes floated. Yogi Basu. She faltered for seconds, dropping the chant. *How?*

Around his dark, all-knowing eyes, his face formed. Her left hand dropped, then reached. His mouth. The gray and brown beard around it. So real.

His lips formed shapes. Words.

Sat Nam. The kundalini rocketed upward. The mirror dropped from her hands. Her whole body tensed in a rictus, a circuit about to blow.

"Shekinah! Breathe! Then let it go. Don't try to hold on!" Whose voice was that? Brenda's?

And her head burst open with a shaft of light. Her tongue spoke words without form. Her arms whirled, spinning worlds into and out of existence.

Shekinah was light. She was truth. She was Lord Shiva, walking now on earth.

51

ALEJANDRO

A low rumble filled the astral plane. If Alejandro hadn't been braced against Tish's back, his stumble would have been a fall. The clattering teeth of the cops snapped, and blood flowed down their chins. The Chief of Police—who was and was not Sheriff Carlson—rose into the air, arms outstretched, turning slowly, hands conjuring.

But the rumbling wasn't coming from there. It came from elsewhere. From Past? No. And here they were in Future. So it must be...

He felt the coven and everyone else gathered. Saw the sigils cycling past, framing the edges of the circle. EYES ON YOU. STRONGER TOGETHER. EYES ON YOU. STRONGER TOGETHER.

And there was the source of the astral shaking seismic roar that built and built in power. Shekinah. In the present. But not on earth. He caught the image of her, multi-armed, brandishing weapons, fierce grin on her face.

Who the fuck?

::*Shiiiiivvvvaaaaaaaa!*:: Tish roared the name of power. It cracked across the astral plane. ::*Om! Namah! Shivaya!*::

Sheriff Carlson's head snapped back as if he'd been punched full force with a massive uppercut.

Tish's sword flamed higher, and she rose into the air, heading straight for Carlson, Police Chief. Alejandro's vision snapped in and out, plane to plane, past, present, future, past.

There was the back room of the Inner Eye. There was the raging bonfire and the horsemen dressed in badly tanned hides. There was Tish's brother, rising up from a puddle of blood on the sidewalk, looking dazed. He held out one hand, pointing to the star on Carlson's chest. *Help*, he mouthed.

::Tish! Watch out!::

Alejandro kicked off and rose into the gray. She needed backup and she needed it now.

SHEKINAH

All must fall before her. Him. Her. Him. All must face the truth about their lives. All must face the moment of reckoning.

All must know how worlds were born and died.

All must know who He was. Dancer of the Worlds. Lord of Light and Fire. Warrior at dawn and lover at dusk. Married to the beautiful, dark-as-night face of Time Herself.

He danced the beginning and the end.

53

ALEJANDRO

He hurtled toward Tish and the Chief of Police, wand and athame both held straight out as if he could pierce Sheriff Carlson's heart. Tish and Carlson faced off. She swiped at him, flames leaping, with the Sword of Truth.

::And the truth shall set us free:: Alejandro sent the thought.

Inside his head, he heard Tish laugh. A hair-raising, terrifying sound. More terrifying than the clattering of teeth from the mute cops down below.

::I can't do this, Alejandro.::

::Yes you can!::

::No. Not what I mean. This is your job. Your destiny. Not mine.::

A burst of anger cracked through his astral form like lightning, filling him with fierce, unwavering, uncompromising Truth.

Fuck.

He knew what he had to do. Alejandro Juan knew. Alejandro Guillermo knew. This was his fucking crisis. The thing about himself he had not wanted to face. The thing he'd fled.

Time caught up with him, and grabbed him by the throat, and time said *Motherfucker. Tell. The. Truth.*

Weeping and moaning, Alejandro skinned his lips back from his teeth and sent a cry through every plane. Through future, past, and present. With the power of his coven and their Gods, and with the strength Shekinah channeled to him in a steady stream.

He caught it in his tools: athame and wand both blazed with heat and light. Blue fire and goldenrod. Sulfur and gold. There was no alchemy that was not his to wield in this time. Right now.

He snapped forward, aiming both his tools at Carlson's neck. The full force of Truth blazed from his tools. He shoved it down the man's throat, until he gagged, struggling, fighting it. Alejandro held his blade at the man's belly and shoved his wand as far down Carlson's throat as it would go.

::Tish! Now!::

::What?::

::Cut the fucking cords from the egregore to its power source! Those police! Doing magic!::

A stink billowed out from Carlson as the Truth ate him alive, inside out. It smelled like burnt hair and blood, and the sick miasma of lifetimes of lies. Alejandro forced every channel in his own astral body open as wide as they would go, letting the full force of the coven and the power of Truth blast through.

The molecules making up his ætheric body felt as if they were being torn apart, the spaces between them shoved wide by the sheer force of the magic pouring through him, setting his nerve endings on fire.

He might not survive this, but if he had to die, in this life and all further lives? He'd make sure Carlson did the same.

::*NO MERCY!*:: he growled as Carlson, eyes rolled back in his head, batted at his arms, struggling, even as the Truth ripped him apart.

::ALL *MERCY!*:: Tish screamed into the widening void. Lifted her flaming sword. And cut.

Carlson caved in like an imploding star, then exploded out with a massive *whoomf* like a propane tank on fire. Alejandro flew backward, desperately clutching his wand and blade.

SHEKINAH

She fell to the carpet, sobbing. Shiva had left her. Shiva had set her free.

"Shekinah!"

"Alejandro!"

Voices. Bustling. Hands. The scents of rose water and lavender.

"Open your mouth." The taste of bitter herbs. Then calm.

ALEJANDRO

The familiar sounds and scents of coven. He coughed and rolled onto his side. His head pounded and his body felt as if he'd just been in a war.

"You're going to be okay." Raquel's voice.

"Tish? Shekinah?"

"They're both fine."

He blinked and pain stabbed through his head. Raquel's face was above him, and he could see Tobias hovering to the side.

"Open your mouth," Tobias said.

He complied, and bitter herbs dropped on his tongue.

"Gah. Can't you make that taste any better?"

Tobias grinned. "Then how would you know it worked?"

"Help me up?"

With Raquel and Tobias's help, he managed to sit upright. Tish was still laid out, flat on the ground, with Tempest and Brenda tending to her. And Shekinah...

His beautiful love was sitting, with Moss at her back and Selene holding her feet. She looked at him and smiled. He mouthed "I love you" at her. She smiled, and mouthed the words back.

Then Thomas was at this side.

"You scared the shit out of me, asshole," the younger man said.

"Yeah," Alejandro replied. "But we did some real magic, didn't we?"

And despite the unsettling nature of that magic, he had to admit...

It felt pretty damn good.

56

SHEKINAH

Shekinah lay in Alejandro's bed, arms wrapped around her lover, listening to him sleep. They'd forgotten to pull the blackout curtains over the privacy sheers the night before, so early morning sunlight filtered through the thin, white curtains. It was going to be a beautiful autumn day.

It was two days after what his coven was already calling "The Ritual of All Time," which had several layers of meaning, of course. She knew that at least some of them hoped that title was an invocation that the intense ritual stuff they'd been dealing with for the past year was done.

The kundalini serpents gently twined up her spine. She breathed in for four counts. Out for four. In for four counts. Out for four. Lord Shiva still buzzed around her head, and the impression she got from that energy was that, though the ritual had done a lot to break the spell of corruption that still held Portland in its sway, the coven's work wasn't done.

And neither was her own.

After the ritual, pretty much everyone involved had collapsed, cared for by the healers among them. The anarchists had seemed excited rather than scared out of their heads, which Shekinah found very interesting. Arrow and Crescent really was something, the way they brought disparate groups together. It was a rare thing that anything united people in that way.

She looked forward to getting to know the Thelemites, heathens, and anarchists better. The whole thing had made her realize how sequestered she'd allowed herself to become. And Yogi Basu agreed.

They'd met the night before, to debrief. He'd seemed unsurprised at what had transpired.

"Of course, Lord Shiva came to you in your hour of need. You think he only lives in the holy books? Now. When will you be ready to start your teacher training?"

Alejandro's breathing changed. She looked down to see a yawn split his beautiful face wide. He'd slept for fourteen hours after the healers had helped her get him home, and had barely stirred since then, except to shower and eat.

And make love to her.

"Hey, love. You finally awake?"

He stretched his arms and she felt him point his toes beneath the comforter. He blinked up at her.

"You know, I think I am. I feel pretty good." He snuggled up higher onto her shoulder, and they lay and breathed together for a while, listening to the distant sounds of the city down below.

"Think you might want to make it outside today?"

"Only if you make hot, naked love to me again."

She laughed and kissed the top of his head. "I think that could be arranged, and since we're both naked right now, it's even convenient."

He stroked her belly, hand warm and delicious.

"You still okay about all this?"

She laughed. "All this'? You mean, getting taken over by

Lord Shiva in the middle of some weird astral ritual with a bunch of witches and anarchists—not to mention my lover's possible new boyfriend—in which the love of my life could have died from magical backlash? Is that the 'all this' you're talking about?"

He scooted all the way up, grabbed a pillow, and leaned against the gray padded headboard next to her. His dark eyes, so playful just a few minutes ago, were serious.

"Yes. All of that. Every bit of it. Plus the fact that you're going to actually start teacher training next week."

"There are things I need to deal with, that's for sure. I feel like my life has been turned up to eleven. But you know..."

She thought about it. Felt it. Felt Lord Shiva. Felt her teacher. Felt the serpents. Felt her lover.

Felt her power.

"It's funny," she said. "Here we thought you were the one having a midlife crisis. But it turns out, I was having one, too. I just had no idea."

"And?"

"And yeah. I'm okay with it. With every last bit."

Shekinah had no idea what tomorrow would bring, but she now knew that, no matter what it was, she was going to be just fine. Better than fine.

She was going to kick ass.

57

ALEJANDRO

He had never loved anyone in his life the way he loved Shekinah right now, and he had loved a lot of people. She sat next to him, blond hair shining in the dappled morning light, face bare, the most beautiful sight he'd ever seen.

"You're one of the bravest people I know."

He felt her shrug. "I don't know about that, but I feel really strong right now. Not questioning myself anymore, you know? How about you?"

He grabbed the steel water bottle from the side table and took a swig, swishing it around his mouth. He still got weird aftertastes from the astral battle. Raquel said they were some sort of psychic cellular memory, and the taste would fade as he integrated the working.

"Other than wanting coffee, I feel pretty good. And yeah, I think I'm ready for whatever is coming now. It came to me in the night, actually."

"What?" she said, slipping out of bed and grabbing one of his T-shirts to shuck on over her head.

"Why are you getting dressed?"

She stood, long legs bare, wicked smile on her face. "You said you wanted coffee, didn't you? Well, the coffee's not going to make itself. I promise we'll get naked again after."

"You really are the best, you know that?" He slipped out of bed himself, pulling on a pair of dark gray sweatpants. They padded companionably to the kitchen space. As Shekinah got the coffee started, he wandered over to the ofrenda. It felt quiet this morning, no longer buzzing with frantic activity and the desperate need to communicate through the thickness of his skull. Come to think of it, the base of his skull felt quiet, too. Tobias had traced some sort of oil at the place where his skull met the top of his spine. He said it would help gently close things down until Alejandro had enough oomph to recalibrate himself again.

"You haven't finished your sentence yet," Shekinah said from beside him. "What came to you in the night?"

The scent of coffee perking filled the room, and his stomach growled. He snaked an arm around her and ignored his stomach. "I'm not going back into corporate IT. I've already got more money than I know what to do with, and minimal expenses."

"So, what are you going to do?" She leaned against his side and they stood, staring at the ofrenda together.

"Not one-hundred-percent sure yet, but I'm sure there are community groups that could use some cheap consulting. And maybe I'll do more with Olivia and the rest of that hacker crew. Do a lot more subversive good than I have been. I'm tired of playing life safe, you know."

Shekinah turned his face, lips meeting his. Goddess, she felt good. He turned in her arms, drawing her closer. They paused for breath, foreheads touching. They breathed together, long and slow, savoring the energy that thrummed between them.

"Which reminds me of something I've been thinking of," Shekinah finally said. "What do you think about getting a little house together? We could have separate bedrooms if we wanted, and we'd both need office space, but..."

"Huh." He turned the thought over in his heart and mind, and found he wasn't afraid of that anymore, either. "How about when Maureen wants to come over? Or Thomas?" He really wanted to spend a lot more time with Thomas. "Or anyone else?"

"Well, the separate bedrooms might be enough...but I was also thinking, we could build a little guest house in the back...for visitors."

He grinned at her. She grinned right back.

"You're talking about a sex shack, aren't you?"

"What else?"

It was his turn to grab her in a kiss. Fuck the coffee, he wanted her. Now.

But before they dragged each other back to the bedroom...

He turned back to the ofrenda.

"Thank you," he said out loud. The ancestors remained quiet.

But he swore the picture of Alejandro Juan winked.

FREE BOOK

If you enjoyed this book, please consider telling a friend, or leaving a short review at your favorite bookseller.

Visit thorncoyle.com for a free short story collection and to sign up for a monthly newsletter.

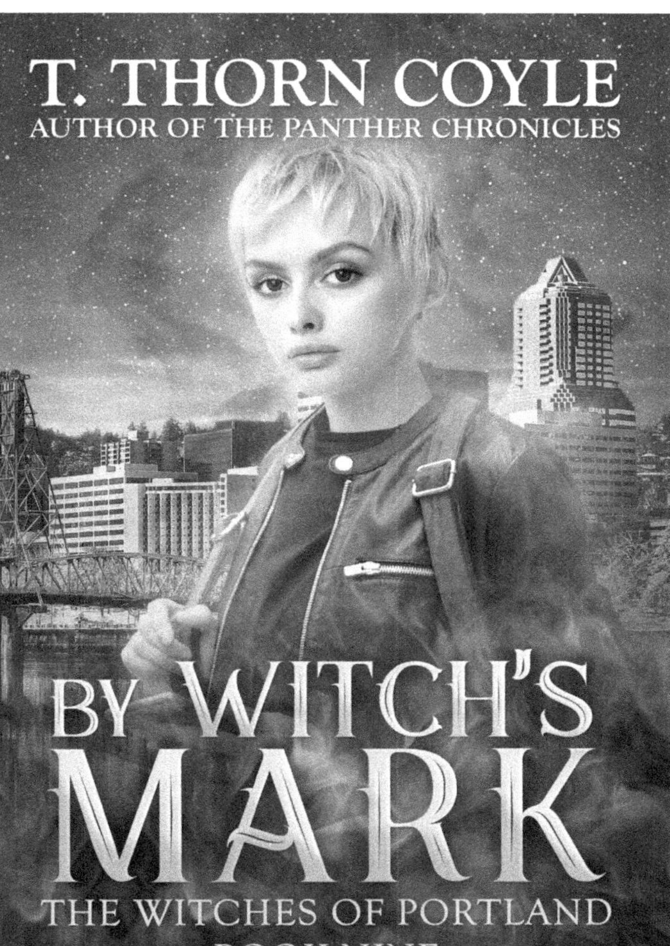

T. THORN COYLE
AUTHOR OF THE PANTHER CHRONICLES
BY WITCH'S MARK
THE WITCHES OF PORTLAND
BOOK NINE

BY WITCH'S MARK

Tempest dug a sharp elbow into a dense knot in Harry's trapezius. Not that the softly snoring man seemed to notice. As usual, Harry was tense and exhausted. The perils of running a small non-profit, she supposed.

A random, chill lounge mix played softly from a speaker in the corner of the dimly lit treatment room, competing with the soft tick of the radiant heater. It was damn cold outside—supposed to snow later in the week—but the room was toasty. Couldn't have the clients getting cold. Tempest appreciated it, too. She was always freezing. She had pushed the long-sleeved black shirt up on her forearms, exposing the tattoos swirling down her right arm. She'd been itching to get more ink and almost had enough saved up. Maybe she'd make an appointment soon. Give herself a solstice gift.

She felt the knot give way. Harry's shoulder finally relaxed, descending from its spot beneath his ear.

Used to be, Tempest envied Harry's ability to sleep, but since her recent foray into using CBD oil, her own sleep seemed to improve. Other things were shifting, too. As the constant exhaustion decreased, she noticed more subtle changes, as if her health itself might just be improving. It was too early to tell—her chronic illness had too many wild variables—but for the first time in ages, she dared to hope.

May Artemis make it so, she thought.

One thing many people didn't know was that Artemis the Hunter was also a healing Goddess, invoked to watch over a parent giving birth.

And she was the fierce protector of children. Tempest was down with that.

Artemis was also the matron Goddess of Arrow and Crescent Coven, and Arrow and Crescent had saved her life. Well, Brenda had, really. Tempest had stumbled into the Inner Eye five years ago now, during a terrible time. She'd just left yet another foster home—not a particularly bad place, but just a place she needed to be free of for... reasons—and was looking for work and a place to crash.

Brenda took one look at Tempest, clucked, and within moments had a cup of tea in her hands and had tucked her into the little Tarot nook at the back of the store with the admonition to not move.

Tempest smiled at the memory and laid a gentle hand on Harry's shoulder. "Time to turn over."

He snorted with a start. "Uh. Yeah."

She lifted the sheet up a foot or so while Harry muscled himself onto his side, then flopped on his back, and scooched himself down on the sturdy table with a big sigh.

"Damn. I swear this is the only time I sleep."

"Then you must need a massage every day." Tempest pumped a shot of oil into her hands and slid her hands under his back to work his trapezius from a different angle.

Harry groaned. "If I could afford the time or money, believe me, I would."

His breathing slowed again as he drifted off.

Tempest deepened her own breathing to match the movements of her hands. She spread her bare toes on the carpet beneath the table and imagined her center of gravity sinking toward the earth. The energy work she'd learned from the coven, coupled with her massage training, were sometimes the only things that allowed her to function at all.

Her health had gotten so bad the past year, her coven members were shooting her worried looks. It worried her, too. There were days when she could barely walk around and it felt as if she was half-drowning. Her brain didn't track and her body didn't want to move.

CBD oil or not, if Tempest couldn't get out of bed, she couldn't work. And that really wasn't good. She'd saved up two months of basic expenses—at her covenmate Alejandro's insistence and backed up by Brenda and Raquel, who wanted her to work on saving even more. Even so, she always knew how close she was to ending up on the streets.

She had been there before, too many times. Running from crappy foster parents after the first wonderful, family had moved out of state for work and couldn't take care of her anymore.

For years, the goodbye tears in their eyes comforted her when it was nowhere else to be found. Someone valued her. That kept her going. And then she found Brenda, and by extension, the coven. So here she was, all these years later, taking care of herself and surrounded by a small group that genuinely seemed to care.

She inhaled deeply, then exhaled and started working on one of Harry's arms. She focused on the scent of almond oil and sent healing energy as deep into Harry's muscles as she could. Being here in this room, doing work she loved, soothed her worries.

But they never seemed to go away.

ACKNOWLEDGMENTS

I give thanks to the cafés of my new hometown, Portland, Oregon. All you baristas are fine human beings.

Thanks also to Leslie Claire Walker, my intrepid first reader, to Dayle Dermatis, editor extraordinaire, and to Lou Harper for my covers. Gratitude to Mark Shekoyan for yoga consultation (any liberties taken are my own) and to my writing buddies for getting me out of the house.

Speaking of house...thanks as always to Robert and Jonathan.

Big, grateful shout out to the members of the Sorcery Collective for spreading the word and to Jack for typo catching.

And last...

Thanks to all the activists and witches working your magic in the world. This series is for you.

Evolutionary Witchcraft

Kissing the Limitless

Make Magic of Your Life

Sigil Magic for Writers, Artists & Other Creatives

Crafting a Daily Practice

ABOUT THE AUTHOR

T. Thorn Coyle has been arrested at least five times. Buy them a cup of tea or a good whisky and they'll tell you about it.

Author of *Steel Clan Saga*, *The Witches of Portland*, and *The Panther Chronicles*, Thorn's multiple non-fiction books include *Sigil Magic for Writers, Artists & Other Creatives*, and *Evolutionary Witchcraft*.

Thorn's work appears in many anthologies, magazines, and collections. They have taught magical practice in nine countries, on four continents, and in twenty-five states.

An interloper to the Pacific Northwest U.S., Thorn stalks city streets, writes in cafes, loves live music, and talks to crows, squirrels, and trees.

Connect with Thorn:
www.thorncoyle.com

www.ingramcontent.com/pod-product-compliance
Lightning Source LLC
Chambersburg PA
CBHW071245190726
48292CB00007B/2414